Rul *Me*

"You can leave your car here for us," Wendy said.

"My *car*?"

"Yes, your car." She chuckled at the look on Luke's face. "This way I'll have something to do the grocery shopping in...."

"You'll use my car to do the *shopping*?" Luke was practically gibbering.

"And then I know you'll come back," Wendy ended serenely. "That is—if you still want me to look after your baby?"

She raised her eyebrows and waited. He glared at her.

"What kind of a bargain is this?" His voice was rising through the roof.

"It's a baby bargain," she told him.

D0779110

PARENTS WANTED

Families in the making!

In the orphanage of a small Australian seaside town
called Bay Beach, there are little children desperately
in need of love. Some of them have no parents,
some are simply unwanted—but each child dreams
about having their own family someday....

The answer to their dreams can also be found in
Bay Beach! Couples who are destined for each other—
even if they don't know it yet—are brought together by love
for these tiny children. Can they find true love
themselves—and finally become a real family?

Look out for the next PARENTS WANTED story
by Marion Lennox
coming soon in Harlequin Romance®.

THEIR BABY BARGAIN

Marion Lennox

PARENTS
WANTED

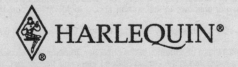

HARLEQUIN®

TORONTO • NEW YORK • LONDON
AMSTERDAM • PARIS • SYDNEY • HAMBURG
STOCKHOLM • ATHENS • TOKYO • MILAN • MADRID
PRAGUE • WARSAW • BUDAPEST • AUCKLAND

If you purchased this book without a cover you should be aware
that this book is stolen property. It was reported as "unsold and
destroyed" to the publisher, and neither the author nor the
publisher has received any payment for this "stripped book."

For all my loopy friends, without whose love and laughter
this book would never have been written.

ISBN 0-373-03662-0

THEIR BABY BARGAIN

First North American Publication 2001.

Copyright © 2001 by Marion Lennox.

All rights reserved. Except for use in any review, the reproduction or
utilization of this work in whole or in part in any form by any electronic,
mechanical or other means, now known or hereafter invented, including
xerography, photocopying and recording, or in any information storage
or retrieval system, is forbidden without the written permission of the
publisher, Harlequin Enterprises Limited, 225 Duncan Mill Road,
Don Mills, Ontario, Canada M3B 3K9.

All characters in this book have no existence outside the imagination of
the author and have no relation whatsoever to anyone bearing the same
name or names. They are not even distantly inspired by any individual
known or unknown to the author, and all incidents are pure invention.

This edition published by arrangement with Harlequin Books S.A.

® and TM are trademarks of the publisher. Trademarks indicated with
® are registered in the United States Patent and Trademark Office, the
Canadian Trade Marks Office and in other countries.

Visit us at www.eHarlequin.com

Printed in U.S.A.

CHAPTER ONE

PEOPLE didn't arrive at Bay Beach Orphanage driving fortunes on wheels. At least, they didn't until now.

Wendy Maher cared for orphans, or for young children from broken homes with no money. Foster-parents tended to spend more on kids than on cars, and orphanage staff did the same.

Therefore Wendy shouldn't even recognise this sports car—a gorgeous deep green Aston Martin DB7 Vantage Volante—much less know its worth. She watched the low-slung car purr into her driveway, and the fact that she could guess almost exactly what it cost was enough to make her blood boil.

Just as it always had at such waste...

She rose stiffly to her feet. A flutter of child's clothes tumbled around her feet, but her attention was no longer on packing. Adam would have killed for a car like this, she thought bleakly. Adam—whose love for expensive cars and fast driving had destroyed more than just himself...

Good grief! What was she doing? She hauled herself back to the present with a jagged wrench. Thinking of Adam still led to heartbreak. She had better things to be thinking of than him.

Like—what on earth was this car doing here? Her Home—one of a series of Homes making up Bay Beach Orphanage—was on a dead-end road. Maybe the driver had turned in by mistake.

'It'll be someone asking for directions,' she told Gabbie. Wendy's five-year-old foster-daughter was also distracted

5

from packing and was now staring out the window at the amazing car. Woman and child gazed at the car together. Then, as he emerged, they gazed at the driver.

The driver was certainly worth a good, long look. He seemed three or four years older than Wendy's twenty-eight years—and he was drop-dead gorgeous! His blond-brown hair was attractively tousled and nicely sun-bleached. He was six feet tall, or maybe a little more. His skin was nicely tanned; he was expensively but casually dressed in cream moleskin trousers and an open-necked, quality linen shirt, and he was wearing the most superb leather jacket.

Or…it was superb if you were into statements of wealth, Wendy thought crossly. Which she wasn't! This man and his car looked like something out of *Vogue* magazine. The cost of the jacket alone would pay more than a month of Wendy's future rent, and the thought made her glower as he strode toward her front door.

Maybe she could charge him to tell him where to go?

The idea made her smile for the first time that day. She touched Gabrielle's flaming curls in a gesture of reassurance, and then crossed to the hall.

'Hello,' she said, swinging the door wide and pinning a smile of greeting on her face that she didn't feel like giving. 'What can I do for you?'

'I hope you can relieve me of a responsibility,' he answered. 'Is this the place where you leave babies?'

Silence.

Wendy stared. The man was smiling like a cover model, he was asking if he could leave a baby *and he was talking as if he was delivering a parcel!* His deep green eyes were twinkling engagingly, and his wide mouth was curved into a matching grin. He looked like a man used to getting his own way, Wendy thought. He had a wonderful smile—a smile to make you do things you had no intention of doing—and it made Wendy back a couple of steps in immediate mistrust.

'I beg your pardon?' she said blankly.

'They told me this was an orphanage,' His smile slipped a little, unsure. 'The sign outside...it says Bay Beach Children's Home.'

He was right. As if to emphasise his point, Gabbie now appeared at Wendy's side. The little girl clung silently to Wendy's skirt, put her thumb firmly in her mouth and stared.

The stranger looked enquiringly from one to another. Together, they were quite a pair—but they didn't match.

Wendy had glossy black curls, twisted casually into a loose knot from which errant wisps were escaping at random. She was tall—five eight or so. She had olive skin, her warm grey eyes were widely set in her open, pleasant face and, although no one could ever call her plump, she was nicely rounded. She was cuddly, her kids decreed—and with her flowery skirt and her soft white blouse she looked as if she'd just stepped out of a mystical Celtic tale.

Wendy looked competent, kind and motherly—an image she'd worked hard to achieve and an image her children approved of very much. Especially Gabbie.

With Wendy assessed, the man looked down at Gabbie. There were few similarities.

Five-year-old Gabbie had startlingly red hair, tied into two short pigtails. Her snub nose was the complete opposite of Wendy's, and her eyes were a deep, fathomless green. Her freckles stood out on her too-pale face; she was finely boned, and she couldn't be any more different from Wendy if she'd tried to be.

This was not a mother-daughter relationship, the man's expression said. He had come to the right place. His smile re-emerged as he faced the *comfortable* Wendy. This lady might not be his sort of woman, but she was who he needed right now.

His confidence had returned with his smile. 'You *are* part of Bay Beach Orphanage,' he announced.

'Yes.' Wendy's hands rested on Gabbie's shoulders as the child's thumb shifted nervously from one side of her mouth to the other. This little scrap was fearful of everything, and Gabbie's biggest fear was always that she'd be snatched from the Wendy she loved. Sadly, it wasn't an unreasonable fear. 'This is a children's home. But in answer to your query…' She took a deep breath. 'You're asking is this the place you leave babies?' Her brows creased together in a frown. Her urge was to slam the door in the stranger's handsome face, but if there was a baby involved then she couldn't do that. 'Do you have a baby?'

'Well, yes,' the man said as if he was apologising. He smiled again. 'I'll bring her in, shall I?'

She followed the man to his car and, with Gabbie still clinging to her side, she waited as the man extricated a bundle from the rear of his fancy car. The infant was in a carry-cot and at least she'd been properly strapped in. In this job she'd seen babies in cardboard boxes—bureau drawers—anything.

But this little one was no neglected waif. The stranger was lifting her—if inexpertly. He was holding her as if she was made of glass, and the baby was a miniature version of himself. She was just beautiful!

She was the most beautiful baby Wendy had ever seen, and Wendy had seen a lot of babies.

The baby had the same soft blond-brown curls as the man, and the same twinkly green eyes, creasing into delight now that she was being lifted. She was wrapped all in pink—there was no possibility of mistaking this little girl for a boy!—and she looked about five or six months old.

And…her eyes said it for her: this was indeed a wonderful world. She was plump and well cared for and happy. Wendy, accustomed to seeing the most awful things that people could do to their children, sighed with relief that at least this baby was healthy.

'I'm leaving tonight—I need to be in New York by the weekend,' the man was saying. He held the baby awkwardly in his arms, proffering her toward Wendy. 'But you'll take care of her, won't you? After all, that's your job.'

There was only one answer to that. 'No,' Wendy said softly, and her eyes met his. Steady and sure, Wendy's were eyes that had seen the worst the world had to offer, and then some. She'd thought nothing could surprise her—but it always did. 'It's not *my* job. Caring for your baby is *your* job.'

'You don't understand.' He was still extending his pink, wrapped bundle, but Wendy wasn't accepting. She held Gabbie's clutching fingers with one hand, and kept her free hand firmly by her side.

'I assume this is your daughter,' she told him. She must be. The likeness was uncanny. 'I'm not sure what's happening here, Mr…'

'Grey. I'm Luke Grey. And, no, she's not my daughter.'

'Mr Grey,' she said and took a deep breath. 'Mr Grey, you don't just dump babies when you wish to go to New York. Or anywhere for that matter.' Her voice was calm and unflappable, her training coming to the fore. 'But you're right. I don't understand. Explain it to me.'

'This is *not* my baby!' But he broke off before he could go any further. Anyone would. An outraged yell from behind them was enough to break off conversations three blocks away.

It was Craig. Of course. Wendy turned to see a small

boy emerge onto the veranda. He was holding a toy fire engine, and his expression said the end of the world had arrived. Right now! Which was nothing unusual. Craig's calamity rate was usually one disaster every hour or so, and he was behind schedule.

'Wendy, Sam broke the hook on my fire engine,' he wailed, his voice still loud enough to announce his catastrophe to the whole of Bay Beach. 'He broke the hook off my crane. Wendy, it's broken…'

'Don't worry, Craig, I have glue,' Wendy called to him, as if broken fire engines were normal. As they were. 'Put it on the kitchen table, and I'll fix it. But first…' she gave Luke's car an appreciative glance, which Luke didn't appreciate at all '…look what's in our driveway,' she told the little boy. 'Call Sam and Cherie, and bring them out to see this man's really nice car.'

Then she managed a tiny internal chuckle as she watched Luke's face go blank in dismay. No matter. Whatever human disasters were around, this car would give her children some pleasure.

It certainly did. The wailing switched off like a tap. *'Wow!'* Stunned, five-year-old Craig stared at the sports car as if it had landed from Mars. 'Is it real?'

'Don't touch it,' Luke said immediately, and Wendy's inner chuckle strengthened. What harm would a few sticky fingers do?

'Bring your baby inside, Mr Grey,' she told him. 'You still need to explain.'

'Will you take her?' he said, and his voice was pleading. He held out his arms. 'She's…she's wet.'

'Babies often are,' Wendy said placidly, still refusing to take his bundle. She led Gabbie up the veranda steps, leaving him to follow, like it or not. 'Okay, we'll change her nappy and then you can tell me all about your problems.

But no, Mr Grey, I won't take her. You carry your baby until I understand what's going on.'

'She's not my baby.'

'That's what you said before.' Seated now in Wendy's kitchen, Luke was still holding his baby. Wendy had changed the little one's nappy and wrapped her in dry blankets but then she'd handed her right back. Now she was making coffee while Luke sat uncomfortably with his beaming bundle and tried not to be distracted by what was happening out the window.

There were three children playing in his car. They couldn't do any real harm, he decided, but he sent up a small prayer anyway. Please... The gorgeous leather upholstery *would* wipe clean...

'So who's baby is she?' Wendy watched where his glance lay, and then dragged his attention back indoors. She handed over a mug of coffee and settled herself. Gabbie made a beeline for her lap and stayed close. Instinctively Wendy's arms came around her and held tight. On Luke's lap, his baby gurgled and chuckled and reached for the mug. There were two adults and two responsibilities. And a whole lot more outside...

'You wouldn't like to get those kids away from my car?' he said uneasily.

'Watch your coffee,' she reminded him. 'Babies burn and she can reach it. You can move your car onto the kerb if you're uncomfortable.' She refused to be ruffled. 'While it's in my yard I can't drag the children away from it.'

'Then will you hold the baby while I shift it?' he begged, and she shook her head.

'No, Mr Grey.' She wasn't taking his baby while he went to move his car. Instinct told her she'd never see him again. And he saw exactly what she was thinking. He stared over the table at her, anger flaring. 'Look, I could have just dumped her and run,' he snapped.

'And you didn't.' She nodded, not warming to the man in the slightest. He might have a smile to knock a girl sideways, but he wasn't coming across well at all. He was a darn sight more worried about his car than his baby. 'That's very noble of you.'

The censure in her tone was obvious, and his brows snapped together in anger.

'You think I'm a rat.'

'It's not my job to think anything of the kind,' she told him. 'I'm paid to worry about children—not to make judgements about the people who are caring for them. Or not caring for them.'

'Hey, *she* was dumped on *me!*'

'Really?' Her grey eyes widened in polite disbelief and she looked from man to baby and back again. 'You know,' she said softly, 'she looks very like you.'

'I'd imagine she does,' Luke said bitterly. 'Of all the stupid…' His eyes flew to Wendy's again, the anger still there. 'But she's not my daughter. I swear.'

'You're related though?'

'I guess we are,' Luke said slowly, and for the first time his attention faded from his precious car. 'I've been thinking.' He cast a dubious look at the little girl he was holding, as if he was still trying to figure out where she'd come from. She'd grabbed a teaspoon; she was banging it on the table, and enjoying the occupation immensely. 'She…she's my half-sister.'

'Your half-sister.' Wendy sat back, had a couple of sips of coffee and hugged Gabbie some more. He'd explain, she guessed. Given time. Meanwhile, Gabbie was still trembling. She'd been trembling all day with the impending move. She needed hugging and Wendy was content to hug her. The rest of the kids had a great new toy to play with—a couple of hundred thousand dollars worth of new toy!—and, despite the fact that she had a train to catch, Wendy wasn't into rushing.

For the baby's sake, she could wait.

'I didn't even know she existed until today,' Luke said bitterly. 'Hell. You're sitting there judging me for dumping her and until this morning I didn't even know I had a half-sister.' His eyes caught hers and held them, willing her to believe him.

And suddenly, unaccountably, Wendy did believe him. His eyes were also demanding she understand. She didn't understand, but she found herself suspending judgement just a little. Her initial vision of playboy father landed with illegitimate baby was put to one side. For the moment.

'Tell me about it,' she said softly. She glanced out the window—just to check. Sam was sitting behind Luke's steering wheel, Craig was in the passenger seat and Cherie was pretending to be the bonnet ornament. They had bare feet, she thought, and no one was wearing belt buckles. They wouldn't scratch his precious car.

But Luke was now not watching his car. He had eyes only for Wendy, trying to make her see.

'It's my father,' he said slowly. 'This is my father's baby.'

Wendy's quick mind mulled this over. Family messes were what she was accustomed to—what she was trained to deal with. 'You mean your father is also this little one's father?'

'I guess.' Luke stared dazedly down at the bundle—who stared back with lively interest. 'She does look like me, doesn't she?'

'She certainly does.' Her voice softened. 'She's the spitting image of you, Mr Grey. Apart from the fact that you're opposite sexes, you're almost identical twins—thirty years apart.'

He stared at the baby for a long moment, trying to take it on board. Finally he shrugged. 'Maybe I need to go back. Explain the whole damned thing.'

'I have time.'

He nodded. This woman really was the most restful person, he thought suddenly. He'd been wallowing in panic ever since he'd opened his door at six this morning. There'd been a knock but when he'd opened the door all he'd found was the bundle. The baby.

Panic? Maybe it wasn't panic, he thought. Maybe panic was far too mild a word for it.

'My father wasn't very reliable,' he said slowly. He took a deep breath, watching her reaction. There wasn't one. Her face was carefully noncommittal and he had the feeling it'd take a lot to shock her. 'Well, maybe that's an understatement. I…I need to be able to make you see. My father had charisma. Anything he wanted, he got. He only had to smile…'

Wendy nodded. She could see that. She just had to look at Luke's smile and she could see that.

'He married my mother,' Luke went on, his smile disappearing completely now and his voice bitter. 'I suppose that's one thing. The marriage lasted for a whole twelve months but at least I was born legitimate. I was the son he always said he wanted, but he wasn't into fatherhood. It cramped his style. When he walked out, my mother went back home—her parents lived on a farm just out of Bay Beach—and I was brought up here. Sort of.'

'Sort of?' She'd never heard of this man, she thought, and she'd been in the district for years.

'Of course, sort of. His son being brought up as a country hick didn't suit my father one bit. To my father, ego was everything,' Luke said bitterly. 'I had to have the best. Despite my mother's protestations, I was sent away to the best boarding schools, and the most prestigious university in Australia. I have no idea how he managed the school fees, and the fact that my mother lived on the breadline didn't worry him a bit. He went from debt to debt. He lied, schemed, swindled—conned his way through life. I didn't know it all. My mother kept it from me and she died when I was twelve, so it's only in the last few years I found out just what his lifestyle was really like.'

'And this baby?'

'This little one was the result of an affair with a woman forty years his junior,' he told her. 'She left a letter this morning, explaining all. Apparently he set her up as he always set up his women—in the height of luxury. He lavished the best on her, and she had no reason to believe there wasn't heaps more cash to come. She became pregnant and had their baby, she must still have been attracting him because he somehow kept supporting her—and then, a month ago, he died.'

Wendy grimaced. 'I'm sorry.'

'Don't be,' he said grimly. 'There was no love lost between my father and me. Once I was old enough to realise how he got his money I never accepted another cent. Lindy, however, depended on him, and I gather she depended on him totally. He's lied to her, he's dead and now she's been evicted from her gorgeous apartment and been left to her own devices.'

'I see.' Wendy couldn't help herself. Her eyes swung to the window again. To the car. And her eyes asked a question.

He got it in one. Understanding flashed into his eyes, and with it, anger. 'I'm a futures broker,' he snapped, following her line of thought exactly. 'So sure, I'm wealthy, but the money I earn is earned honestly. It's nothing to do with my father.'

'But you're not sharing? With, who did you say, Lindy?'

'I've hardly had a chance,' he snapped. 'Even if the idea of supporting my father's mistress appealed to me—which it doesn't—I wasn't asked. I was overseas when my father died and I had no idea Lindy even existed. There's been no contact between me and my father for years. I paid for the funeral and I thought that was it. Then today…'

'Today?'

'Lindy must have known about *me,*' he said bitterly. 'Maybe my father told her I existed and she came looking. Anyway, this morning the baby was dumped in her carry-cot in my lobby. The note Lindy left also said that she only had the baby because my father was so persuasive—he must have been having a late-life crisis or something. But now there's no money she has no intention of staying saddled with a daughter. So she's leaving. The baby's all mine, the note said.'

All yours…

Wendy gazed across the table at Luke and he gazed back. Take this problem away from me, his eyes pleaded.

And those eyes… His father's eyes… They could persuade a woman to do anything, she thought. They'd persuaded a young woman to have a baby she didn't want. They could persuade *her*…

No! She needed to harden her heart.

Blood ties were the most important link a baby could have, Wendy knew. That truth had been drilled into her over and over, all through her career as a social worker. Maintain family links at all costs. Sever those links only if the child is in dire peril.

This baby was sitting on her half-brother's lap, banging her spoon and chirruping as if the world was her oyster.

She had a great big brother. Healthy, wealthy and secure, he could easily support her. If Wendy could swing it, this baby was set for life.

'I assume you don't live in Bay Beach now,' she said softly, thinking hard as she spoke.

'No. I have an apartment in Sydney and another in New York. I move around.'

'You've driven this little one here—all the way from Sydney?'

He seemed a bit disconcerted at that. 'Yes.'

'Can I ask why?' She hesitated, watching his face. 'There are child care services in Sydney. You just had to look up the phone book to find one.'

'I sort of wanted—'

'You sort of wanted—what?'

He looked up and stared at her, his eyes blank. 'Hell,' he said at last. 'It's hard.'

'I can see that.'

'What's your name?' he asked suddenly, and she smiled.

'Sorry, I should have said. It's Wendy. Wendy Maher.'

'Well, Wendy...' He shook his head, his look still confused. On his lap his tiny sister had let her spoon fall sideways. She was squirming into his chest, and her dark little lashes were fluttering downward. He must have stopped along the road and fed her, Wendy thought. She was fed and warm and sleepy. Unconsciously Luke's arms held her close as she nestled into him, and Wendy's eyes warmed at the sight. Maybe...

'I knew there was an orphanage here,' he told her. 'I remembered it and rang—to make sure it still existed. As a child I spent some time in the original Home under I guess what you'd call respite care, when my mother was ill and my grandparents couldn't cope.'

'I see.'

'And…' he was desperately trying to make her understand '…Bay Beach is a great place to grow up.'

'It is at that.' Damn. That hurt. Wendy's grip tightened on Gabbie. She couldn't give a Bay Beach upbringing to Gabbie, she thought bitterly, much as she'd love to. Still, a stable home had to be better than a specific location.

'The best time in my life was when I lived here as a child,' Luke continued, watching her face as if he was trying to guess her thoughts. 'When my mother and my grandparents were alive it was great. The beach! The freedom!' He gestured to the children outside. 'These kids…they're lucky.'

Yeah, right. He needed to pull the wool from his eyes on that one. Dumping his sister and running, and then telling himself it was all for the best because Bay Beach was a great place to grow up…

'No, Mr Grey, these children aren't lucky,' she said firmly. 'These children have problems. They don't have parents who care for them. For now, these children are alone in the world. I'm a paid child care worker, and they only have me or those like me.'

There was a long, drawn out silence. In Luke's arms, his tiny sister finally closed her eyes, nestling back into his chest with absolute trust.

Trust…

He stared across the table at Wendy. This woman was still young, he thought, but she was a far cry from the women he spent his free time with. She was a world away from them. There was warmth in her eyes, and compassion and caring. She could be beautiful, he thought. With a little make-up—a modern hairstyle—some decent clothes…

No!

She was beautiful now, he decided. She needed none of those things.

Why?

It was indefinable. He looked into the calm, grey depths of those luminescent eyes and he knew, despite what Wendy said, that these kids were lucky. Sure, they had dreadful problems, but in the midst of their crises, they'd found Wendy.

'It'll do for my sister,' he said softly. 'If that's all there is. Her mother's abandoned her, but there's no one I'd rather leave her with than you.'

CHAPTER TWO

IT WASN'T going to happen.

He had his solution all mapped out, Wendy thought, looking across the table at him. Ha! She stared at him with trouble in her eyes and, as she tried to find words to reply, there was a thump on the door and a woman burst into the kitchen. It was Erin. Running late, as usual.

Like Wendy, Erin was in her late twenties, but unlike Wendy she was blonde, she was bouncy and she appeared supremely unfrazzled by life. She beamed at Wendy, and held up her hands in apology.

'Sorry I'm late. You must have been panicking. I had to take Ben Carigan to placement. But what on earth is happening? That is the *best* car in your driveway! Fabulous. I've never seen such a car. Don't tell me you've found someone to drive you to Sydney? But if you have, where are you going to put the luggage? There's never room…'

Then she paused for breath, realised Wendy wasn't alone and she turned her high-beam smile on to Luke. 'Oh, hi. Sorry…'

Then she checked out Luke's baby. Her effervescence faded and she glanced again at Wendy, her smiling eyes asking a question.

Erin was a Home mother, too, and Home mothers had rules. They didn't interrupt. The kitchen tables of the Homes that made up Bay Beach Orphanage saw heaps of emotion, and both Wendy and Erin were trained to deal with it. And they were also trained to disappear when it was right to disappear. 'You want me to go and haul children off your gear stick?' she asked, backing to the door. 'Craig's trying his best to unscrew it.'

'No.' Wendy shook herself, as if she was coming out of a dream. This wasn't her job. Not any more. 'I need to move.' She gave Gabbie a swift hug, set her on her feet and rose herself. 'Mr Grey, this is Erin Lexton, our new Home mother. Erin, this is Mr Luke Grey, and this little one is his half-sister.' She stood, considering the pair of them, and then motioned to the sleeping baby. 'By the way, you didn't say. Does your sister have a name?'

'It's Grace,' Luke said, also rising. 'Her name is Grace.'

'It's a very pretty name,' Erin said, her intelligent eyes taking everything in. 'Your...half-sister, did Wendy say?'

'Yes.'

'Luke's asking us to take Grace in and care for her,' Wendy told her. 'I was about to tell him it's impossible.'

'It sure is.' Erin smiled apologetically and shrugged. 'We're full to bursting. As soon as Gabbie and Wendy leave, I have twins coming in. They're eight years old, and trouble personified. I've had them before when their unfortunate mother's had enough. That counts me out for taking any more, and the other Homes are packed as well. Mary and Ray have room for another one, but their Home's for teenagers. Mary hasn't done mothercraft.'

Then she frowned, subjecting Luke to a really close stare. 'Pardon me for saying this...' She looked from Luke to Wendy and back to Luke again. 'With that car, if you can't look after your sister yourself, then surely you can afford a nanny to care for her. Surely you don't need welfare.'

'Which is just what I was about to tell Mr Grey when you arrived,' Wendy agreed. 'The cost of replacing a tyre for that thing out there...' she couldn't quite keep the disdain from her voice '...would pay a nanny for a month.

There are nanny agencies in Sydney, many of them excellent. We can even recommend one for you.'

Luke's brow snapped down in distaste. 'I don't want her to stay in Sydney. Not with hired help.'

Wendy sighed. Oh, dear... However, this was not her problem. None of this was her problem. Erin was walking in, she was walking out, and her time as Home mother at Bay Beach was over.

'Erin, Mr Grey has been landed unexpectedly with his half-sister,' she told her replacement. 'He needs help—assistance in locating the child's mother, counselling, social services maybe. Could you ring Tom at head office and organise him an appointment?' She managed a smile at Luke, took Gabbie's hand and forced herself to go on. Leaving was the hardest thing. To walk away...

She must. For Gabbie.

'I'm afraid I don't work here any more,' she said softly. 'I'm sorry, Mr Grey, but Erin is Home mother here now. If you'll excuse us, Gabbie and I have a train to catch.'

'No!' It was a sharp order from one accustomed to command, and Wendy raised her eyebrows in polite enquiry as Luke rose to his feet and snapped out the word.

'No?'

'Just what I said. No! What do you mean, you're leaving?' Luke reached forward, took her hand and held on. He was like a drowning man who'd been thrust a stick to pull him to shore, only to have someone try and snatch it away again. 'You can't. I want you to look after my sister.'

Wendy looked down at their linked hands, a tiny frown creasing between her eyes. It felt...odd. This was her job, she told herself. She'd had parents clutch her before.

It didn't normally feel like this.

'Mr Grey, Wendy has resigned,' Erin said softly, her eyes darting back and forth. She knew what Wendy was going through—who better?—and she knew that Wendy needed to leave, but there was something about Luke Grey...

Apparently Wendy was nothing to do with this man—Erin's first wild hope that a wealthy boyfriend had arrived out of the murky past had been unfounded—and it was against the rules to break confidentiality.

But then, Erin didn't necessarily follow formal rules. Her sharp mind was working overtime. She'd been worrying about her friend for weeks, and suddenly there seemed a glimmer of an answer. If she could swing it...

'Mr Grey, Wendy's taking Gabbie on as a permanent foster child,' she told him, ignoring Wendy's sharp intake of breath. 'Gabbie's mum won't have her adopted. She keeps taking her back—but often for only weeks at a time—and every time Gabbie returns she has to be placed wherever there's room. Wendy's decided she wants to be available full-time for Gabbie—so every time her birth mum abandons her she can always go back to Wendy.'

'Oh, for heaven's sake...' Wendy managed. She gave Erin a stunned look. 'Erin—'

'And she's burned out,' Erin retorted, ignoring Wendy completely. She was focused solely on Luke, and she was fighting for her friend. 'She's had years of saying goodbye to kids and it's got to her. Apart from what happened before she came here... Anyway, it's taken its toll, so she's opted out. Starting now. The only problem is, Wendy has little money. Because of high holiday rentals there's nowhere in Bay Beach she can live cheaply and there's no work here except what she's doing now. She's spent every spare cent she's ever earned on her kids. So she's taken a one-room apartment in Sydney, which'll be the pits.'

'Erin, this is none of Mr Grey's business,' Wendy expostulated. 'I can't—'

'Isn't it?' Erin smiled suddenly, and there were machia-vellian lights twinkling in her eyes. Honestly—the woman was incorrigible. 'Isn't it just?' She turned back to Luke and she beamed. 'I've suddenly had the best solution! You're saying you need someone to care for your baby, and you want that someone to be Wendy. Wendy needs a pay packet. Ideally she wants to stay here. At Bay Beach—'

'Erin, stop!' Wendy was ready to throttle her. 'I can hardly stay here,' Wendy retorted. 'There's nowhere to rent—even if I could afford it.'

'Yes, there is.' Luke's voice came out of nowhere—al-most as if he hadn't meant it to happen—and both women stared at him.

'I beg your pardon?' Wendy was so far out of her depth she didn't know whether she was hearing right. Erin had just exposed far more than she'd wanted her to expose. Why? This man had nothing to do with her.

But apparently Luke had other ideas.

'I have a place you can have rent-free,' Luke told her. 'You take care of my little sister, Wendy Maher, and I'll give you a home in Bay Beach for however long you want it.'

You could have heard a pin drop. No one spoke at all.

Amazingly, even the bubbly Erin was silent. She was just plain stunned. She'd thrown the embryo of an idea into the air, and suddenly a miracle was happening.

Erin talked all the time but she knew when to shut up. She shut up now.

'I...' Wendy pushed a couple of errant curls from her eyes and tugged her hand away from Luke. Luke was still holding it, and he didn't let her go now. 'Please.' She tugged again. 'I have a train to catch.'

'To a one-room apartment in Sydney when you want to stay here? And how are you going to make a living?'

'I can get a job in child care while Gabbie's at school.'

'You know darn well those types of jobs are like hen's teeth,' Erin retorted—and then subsided at the look in her friend's eyes. Oh dear—maybe she had gone too far.

'I'll pay you well,' Luke told Wendy. This was a man accustomed to making fast decisions and he'd made one now. 'Your friend's right. I can afford to pay for a nanny. I'll check out the going rate and pay you more. Plus living expenses. You can live at the farm.'

'The farm?'

'I have a farm.' He smiled and took pity on the look of sheer bewilderment on her face. His hand holding hers pressed it gently, and then he released her fingers. She let her hand fall to her side, but she looked down at it, as if it still contained...

What? She didn't know. Some trace of future trouble? Something she didn't understand at all.

'I told you my grandparents owned a farm outside Bay Beach,' he told her. 'Well, it's just south of here and it's gorgeous. There's two hundred acres of prime grazing land, with beachfront and the river forming the northern boundary. When they died they left it to me—in trust so my father couldn't get his hands on it. Because I loved it so much, I've never sold it. It's been let for agistment—a local farmer runs his cattle on it—but the house is still there and it's empty. If you want it, it's yours.'

'If I want it?' Wendy stared at him as if he'd lost his mind. A farm. Here! *If* she wanted it....

'Of course she wants it,' Erin said briskly. 'Just say yes, Wendy.' She fixed her friend with a steely look. 'Say yes, dope. Fast!'

'No!' Wendy shook her head. By her side, Gabbie was still watchful. Wary. Reminding her to be careful. The world had kicked this little one around too much for Wendy to take any more risks on her behalf. An inner voice was screaming at her to be careful.

'Where did you say the farm was?' she asked.

'Two miles out of town.' Luke let his eyes crease into his accustomed smile. Finally this mess looked like getting sorted.

'What was your grandparents' name?'

'Brehaut.'

'The Brehaut place!' Wendy stared, and Erin let her breath out in a gasp of excitement.

'Oh, it's gorgeous. The Brehaut farm…'

'That house hasn't been lived in for twenty years,' Wendy said, puzzled. 'No one could ever figure out why.'

'And now we know,' Erin said exultantly. 'Isn't it the most exciting thing?'

'Is it liveable?'

'Yes, I think so.' A trace of uncertainty entered Luke's eyes. 'I keep it maintained. The farmer who uses the land keeps it weatherproof.'

'Weatherproof isn't the same as liveable.'

'Oh, for heaven's sake, Wendy,' Erin snapped. 'You can fix the place.'

'While I care for a baby and a five-year-old.' Wendy shook her head. 'Mr Grey—'

'Luke.'

'Luke, then.' She met his look head on, steel meeting steel. On the surface this offer seemed too good to refuse, but Gabbie was by her side and Gabbie was why she'd thrown in a perfectly good career and was moving on.

'It'd include Gabbie?' she asked. 'I'd have the run of the house and Gabbie could stay with me?'

'The house has five bedrooms,' he said, expanding on his theme, and worry fading by the minute. This was looking better and better. Over the years he'd fretted about the farm, knowing he should sell it, but always he'd held back. Sentiment, he guessed, though he told himself it was a reasonable investment. Now, if Wendy was to fix it up a bit... Make it a home...

'You'd set it up legally?' she asked.

'Watertight,' he told her. 'I need to go to New York tonight, but I'll send my lawyer down from Sydney. I'll instruct him to do whatever necessary to have you stay.'

Wendy blinked. There had to be a catch. Somewhere.

She looked at the baby sleeping in Luke's arms. Grace. Grace and Gabbie. She'd be caring for two little girls...

This could be perfect. This way, if—*when*—Gabbie's mother demanded time with her daughter there wouldn't be such a hole in her life. She'd remain busy doing what she loved best, and there'd still be a home waiting for Gabbie when she returned.

But the house hadn't been lived in for how many years? And the unknown factor—this new little baby's mother—could return at any minute, and reclaim her baby. She'd only dumped her this morning. There was all the reason in the world to suppose she'd change her mind, and where would that leave Wendy and Gabbie?

No! There were dangers everywhere she looked, and if she didn't catch this train—when did it leave?—oh, good grief, in less than an hour!—she'd be too late to get the keys to her new apartment. She'd lose it and she'd be stuck with nowhere to live in Sydney.

On the other hand, if she agreed and took two small children out to a derelict farm, and Luke headed back to New York...

She'd be stuck, she thought wildly. She could be in the biggest mess, and it wasn't just her. It would be Gabbie and Grace as well. She had no legal right to take on the responsibility for this baby. She wondered whether Luke did. Probably not. So it had to be said.

'No,' she said firmly, and bit her lip as she heard herself say it. It was such a glorious idea. To say no was dreadful—but she had to be sensible.

'Wendy!' Erin wailed.

'May I ask why not?' Luke was in businessman mode here—moving in organisational capacity. This was what he was good at. 'It's a very good offer.'

'It may be an exceptional offer,' she told him. 'But if the farm's a wreck then it's not. Or if I'm accused of taking Grace when I have no legal right to care for her. I'll bet you haven't even thought of the legal ramifications of guardianship. Have you?'

His eyes went blank. Clearly he hadn't. 'No.'

'Then, I thank you for your very kind offer,' she said firmly. 'But I can't accept. Unless...'

'Unless?'

'Unless you postpone your trip to New York. Unless you spend enough time with us at the farm to ensure it's liveable, and you don't leave for New York until everything's legally settled and I'm happy that the children have a secure and reasonable place to live.'

He didn't like it.

For the next ten minutes Luke produced every argument he could think of to have her change her mind. At the end of the ten minutes she simply took Gabbie's hand and led her from the room.

'We have a train to catch,' she reminded him simply. 'I'm pushed for time. Goodbye, Luke.'

Goodbye...

Balked, he glared after her but it made no difference. The kitchen door swung closed behind her and he glared at Erin instead.

'She's right,' Erin said helpfully. Sadly but helpfully. 'Wendy needs the legal rights to care for your baby, and she doesn't have them. And if no one's lived in that place for twenty years it'll be a mess. You know it. Kids need safe places to live.'

'I need to be in New York.'

'Then, you have different priorities,' she told him. 'When do you plan on leaving?'

'Now. Tonight. Midnight if I can get back to Sydney on time.'

'And what do you plan on doing with Grace?'

'She's not my responsibility,' he said helplessly, staring down at the sleeping baby in his arms.

'In that case leave her with our children's services and they'll find placement for her in Sydney.' Erin tilted her chin. She was taking a big risk and she knew it. She held her breath.

He glared at her some more.

And then he looked down at the child in his arms and his glare sort of died.

'I...'

'You don't want to do that, do you?' Erin asked gently.

'No.'

'What's so important in New York?'

'Meetings. I'm a broker.'

'I'll bet you have the internet and e-mail and all sorts of other technological gadgetry to overcome this crisis,' she said brightly. 'Teleconferencing, maybe? I hear it's all the go. We even use it here to link up with our Sydney offices.'

He glowered. 'I'll bet there's not even a phone at the farm.'

'Which is one reason Wendy is right in saying she can't agree to live there yet. You don't have a mobile phone?'

'Of course I have a mobile, but...'

'There you go, then.' She smiled again, all objectives achieved. 'I'd stop her packing, if I were you,' she said kindly. 'Once she gets on that train you'll have lost the greatest nanny a man could ever hire. Wendy's simply the best.'

And Luke, staring down at her bright smile, knew that it was true. He knew instinctively that in Wendy he had someone he wouldn't mind entrusting a baby he cared for.

Cared for?

He didn't care for Grace.

But... He stared down at the sleeping baby, and his tiny half-sister stirred in his arms and snuggled closer.

'Hell!'

'It is, isn't it?' Erin said sympathetically. 'Or it will be if you don't stop Wendy from boarding that train. New York or Wendy, Mr Grey. You choose—but choose now.'

'Hell!' he said again.

'Swearing won't help,' she said sweetly. 'Choosing will.'

An hour later, Wendy was in the front passenger seat of an Aston Martin sports car, being driven south.

Against her better judgement.

She should be on a train to Sydney right now, she told herself. That was the place for sedate foster parents. If she was on a train, the wind wouldn't be blowing in her hair, she'd have all her suitcases in the luggage racks above her head, and she'd have Gabbie safely on her knee.

Now the wind was very definitely blowing in her hair and her unruly knot was almost completely unwound. Her luggage was back at Bay Beach—there was no chance it'd fit into Luke's miniscule baggage compartment and he'd organised a taxi to bring it out later. Grace was in her carry-cot, and Gabbie was sitting in the car's rear seat with her mouth as wide open as her eyes. She looked in a state of shock.

Which just about summed up how Wendy was feeling.

'I've been bamboozled,' she said faintly. 'I don't have a clue what I'm doing here.'

'That makes two of us,' Luke said, not without sympathy. 'I should be heading for the airport right now.' He shifted his hands on his steering wheel and grimaced. 'There's something sticky on this.' Then he stared down with horror as he saw two grey marks on his leather steering wheel. 'Someone's touched this with sticky hands!'

Good grief, Wendy thought blankly. After all that was happening, the man was worrying about a sticky steering wheel!

'It'll wash off,' she said shortly.

'You're sure?'

'Oh, for heaven's sake, it's only red jelly. The kids had red jelly for lunch. It dissolves in warm water.'

'There's red jelly on my steering wheel,' he groaned. And then he looked closer. It wasn't red. It was definitely grey.

'How can this be red jelly?'

'It's red jelly mixed with things.' She had the temerity to grin. 'Hey, I said they had red jelly for lunch. That was two hours before you arrived. They did things after that. playdough. Mud. Finger paints…'

'I don't want to know!'

Silence. He could feel her disapproval from the other side of the car—as if she thought this was some huge piece of ostentation.

'You like your car, then?' she said cautiously, and he managed a smile. Okay, maybe it would wash off.

'Wouldn't you? She's gorgeous. If you knew what she cost me, first and last—'

'I could make a very good guess what she cost you,' Wendy said tartly. 'Aston Martin Vantage Volante. Whew! She's worth a fortune.'

'You don't know—'

'I'll bet I do know. To within ten thousand dollars or so, anyway, and, with a car like this, what's ten thousand dollars?' She grimaced. 'What else could I guess about this car?' She thought it through, and Adam's tones of reverence were still with her. 'I'd guess it has an all-alloy, quad cam, forty-eight valve, twelve cylinder engine? Zero to sixty miles per hour in approximately five seconds. Top speed of about a hundred and sixty miles an hour. Yes, she's some plaything, Mr Grey.'

'How the heck…?'

'And if you knew what I could do with a quarter of the money this car cost you—'

'Hey, I'm your employer,' he interrupted. 'You're not here to give me moral lectures!'

'Let me out, then,' she said serenely. 'Moralistic lectures come with the package.'

For a moment she almost thought he would. His foot eased from the accelerator, and then Grace gurgled from her carry-cot in the back seat and the impossibility of dumping this woman anywhere hit home.

'Where did you learn about cars?' he asked grudgingly, and she wrinkled her nose. In truth it was sort of nice to have the warm sea air blowing through her hair and a gorgeous leather seat enfolding her, but she wouldn't admit it for the world.

'My ex-husband was a car fanatic.'

'Oh.' He looked sideways at her. 'You're divorced?'

'He's dead.'

There was something about the way she said it that precluded any more questions. Back off, her tone said, and he had the sense to do just that.

'Right.'

'You're not married?'

'No.' He grinned and looked sideways at her. 'I decided early to love cars instead. They're cheaper.'

'Oh, sure.' She took a deep breath. 'Mr Grey, do you have any idea what you're letting yourself in for? In one day, you've assumed responsibility for one baby, you've hired a nanny, you've agreed to accommodate another child…'

'It's no great shakes,' he said. 'I can afford it. Just as long as none of you cause me any bother.'

'And if we do?'

'Then I'm out of here.' His grin deepened. 'I will be anyway. Emotional attachment is not my style. I'll get the legalities all drawn up and then I'll leave.'

'Just as long as the house is liveable.'

'It will be.'

It wasn't.

The house hadn't been entered for twenty years. It was like turning back a time machine, Wendy thought wonderingly. With Gabbie still pressed by her side she walked from room to room. Luke walked beside her carrying Grace, and he didn't speak either.

The house was ghostlike. Windows had been broken and boarded up. Furniture was covered with dustsheets, and cobwebs hung in vast nets draped from the ceiling. Underneath it all, the house was big and gracious and old, and the furniture was of quality, but the curtains had disappeared into moth-eaten shreds, the carpets were threadbare and the dust lay in blankets over everything. Wendy's nose wanted to sneeze the minute Luke opened the door.

They walked from room to room in stunned silence. It was a piece of history that time had forgotten, and its ambience almost overwhelmed her. How much more must it stun Luke, Wendy thought, when the house was full of memories—of how it had been when he'd been a boy?

There were photographs everywhere, and most of them were of Luke. There were frames of Luke as a baby, looking just like Grace. A cobwebbed portrait hung on the wall—it surely must be Luke as a chubby toddler, grinning from his mother's knee. The woman who held him, even then, showed weariness, defeat and traces of illness on her face, and Wendy found herself wondering how she'd died.

There were more. She lifted a frame from a carved side table and blew away the dust, and there was Luke at about five years old. He was standing between an elderly couple and they were holding his hands with pride. Even covered with dust, the love shone through.

No wonder Luke had kept this place, Wendy thought. No wonder he'd instinctively brought Grace here. He might have been packed off to boarding school, but here, even dust-coated and tattered, this place had been his home.

And maybe it still was. She glanced sideways and caught the look that flashed across his face—and it was a look of raw pain.

'Apart from the dustsheets and window boarding, it's hardly been touched since they took my grandmother to hospital,' Luke said at last. He was speaking in a hushed whisper—it was that sort of place.

'It must have been a beautiful home.'

'As you said, though,' he said sadly, 'it's uninhabitable now.'

'Not quite.' Wendy braced her shoulders and looked down at Gabbie. 'We like a challenge, don't we, Gabbie?'

'Is this where we're going to live?' Gabbie asked in a

quavering voice and Wendy picked her up and hugged her close.

'Yes. Absolutely. And it's going to be the best home that girls like us could ever ask for. Underneath all this dust it's *beeyootiful!*'

'We need to stay at a hotel tonight,' Luke said doubtfully. 'Maybe if we put in a team of cleaners and carpenters...' He could see his trip to America being postponed indefinitely. Damn, this had seemed such a good idea. But now...

Wendy was shaking her head. 'No. This is fine—better than I thought it might be. We don't need to move any more. Gabbie spends her life moving, don't you, Gabbie? If this is home, then it's home from now on.'

She walked over to the window—they were standing in what must be the formal living room—grabbed a board from the window and pulled. The board broke free, a rush of warm salt air flowed into the musty room and outside she could see...

'The sea!' Wendy said exultantly. 'Look, Gabbie, the sea!' Beyond the wide, gracious veranda, across a paddock where Hereford cattle gazed in placid contentment under the shady gums, lay the sea. From here it looked as if there was a sandy beach, maybe even safe for swimming. It looked—wonderful!

'The sea, the sea, the sea!' Wendy lifted Gabbie and swung her round and round, delight shining from her eyes. She wasn't sure how this had happened, but this was a dream! 'We're going to love living by the sea, Gabbie, love. Any time your mum doesn't want you, then you'll live here with me. By the sea. In this house which is going to be the most wonderful place on God's earth.'

Then she set Gabbie firmly down, fixed her with a grin,

hauled up her sleeves and turned to eye Luke with a speculative gleam.

'All it needs is work.'

'Hey, I'm a futures broker,' Luke said in an alarmed voice, seeing the thoughts running riot behind the gleam. 'I'm not a cleaner.'

'And I'm a social worker, and Gabbie is a five-year-old ward of the state. But, as of now, we're all of us cleaners. Needs must, Mr Grey. Gabbie, let's choose you a bedroom first, and we'll clean that out from stem to stern. Because Gabbie's bedroom is the most important room in this house.'

'Hey!'

'Yes?' Wendy raised her eyebrows politely at Luke. 'You don't agree?'

'We can hire cleaners.'

'Not tonight we can't. We're the cleaners. If you want us to make this a home, then you need to put some effort into it. Like now!'

'I'm not dressed for it.' He stared down at his leather jacket and immaculate trousers and Wendy grinned.

'And you have lesser clothes at home? Go on, Luke Grey. Surprise me. Tell me you have old, paint-stained overalls in your garage—from all that odd jobbing you do at weekends.'

He had the grace to give a half-hearted smile. 'Well, maybe not.'

'So these clothes maybe aren't your best clothes?'

He thought of his designer suits. 'Hell, no.'

'See, it could have been worse,' she said cheerfully, arranging Grace's carry-cot carefully in a dust-sheeted armchair and covering it with a shawl. 'There you go. Your baby's safe and sleeping, and it's time for the rest of us to work. Gabbie's room first.'

'I thought…' he was so stunned he could hardly get his voice to work '…the kitchen, maybe.'

'We have children, Luke Grey,' she said softly. 'Get your priorities right. We need a fire—outside I think, because it's my bet the chimney's blocked and we need hot water. It'll take a brave person to tackle that fire stove, and maybe I'm not the person to do it. At least not tonight. And if I'm not brave enough, I'm darned sure that you're not. Bailing out to a hotel! Goodness, what a wimp! Right, Luke. Right, Gabbie. Let's get this house habitable.'

If anyone had told Luke when he'd woken that morning that instead of flying to New York he'd spend the afternoon and evening on his knees with a scrubbing brush and a nose full of dust and cobwebs, he'd have told them they were dreaming.

But that's just what was happening. Wendy didn't let him off the hook for a minute. While Grace snoozed, she set them to work like there was no tomorrow and, with the wimp label ringing in his ears, he gritted his teeth and did it.

The room Gabbie chose was miniscule—a tiny boxroom added on to the end of the house. Its windows looked out over the ocean almost all the way to Hawaii, but that wasn't why she'd chosen it.

'You tell me where you're sleeping,' she'd demanded of Wendy, and Wendy had nodded and had carefully chosen the room with an adjoining door. To the boxroom…

'We'll be able to sleep with our doors open and talk,' Gabbie had whispered and Luke had wondered not for the first time what was behind this little girl's terror.

Not that he'd had time for much wondering. 'We're not going to bed until we have Gabbie's room perfect,' Wendy decreed, and while he scrubbed she was marching outside with linen and blankets and rugs and curtains to hang over the ancient clothes line. She armed Gabbie with a broom, she used a bigger one herself, and together they thumped them free of generations of dust.

They aired them in the sea breeze, they inspected Luke's handiwork and then Wendy graciously approved the return of her cleaned soft furnishings. She had Gabbie marching in and out with pillows on her head—and giggling. She had Luke scrubbing as if his life depended on it. Even Grace slept as if she'd been ordered to.

This wasn't a boss-employee kind of relationship, Luke thought grimly as he scrubbed. Or if it was, he knew who was the boss. And it wasn't him!

Finally, however, Wendy called a halt.

'Okay. We have one bedroom and one living room sorted. Kind of. Now, it's dinnertime.'

'Dinner…' Luke sat back on his heels—he'd been scrubbing skirting-boards and wiping out a spider's nest—and regarded his handiwork with a kind of detached pride. Gabbie's bedroom did look good. They'd unboarded the two unbroken windows—it'd look a whole heap better when they'd had a glazier in—but you could see the sea, and in every other way it looked just as it had twenty years back.

He'd slept in here sometimes, he remembered. His official bedroom had been one of the bigger front ones, but the room adjoining this had been his mother's and sometimes he'd crept in here to sleep when he'd been ill, or when his mother had been ill and he'd worried, or in the days before he'd had to leave again for boarding school…

He'd chosen this room because he loved it, and he'd lain here at night while he and his mother had talked until he'd slept. This was the best…

Oh, for heaven's sake! He shook his train of thought

away with anger. How long since he'd been sentimental like this?

But the bed was made up again with a patchwork quilt he remembered his mother and grandmother making, and there was a painting on the faded yellow wall that he remembered his grandfather buying...

Grandpa would like Gabbie sleeping under that painting, Luke decided, and then caught Wendy looking at him with a strange expression on her face. It was as if she could see what he was thinking.

She didn't let on. Instead she teased him with a smile. 'Resting on your laurels, Mr Grey?'

'I don't see why I shouldn't,' he retorted, stung. 'I certainly deserve to.' He held up his hands. 'Look. Blisters! I have housemaid's hands, lady. And—'

'And?'

'I'm hungry.'

He was, too, he realised. Starving. But there was no food in the house.

'That's all fixed.' Her smile intensified, and he gazed up at her in astonishment. She really was the most extraordinary woman! 'I've taken the liberty—'

'*Another* liberty!' He groaned, struggled to his feet and held up his hands in mock horror. Hell, he had housemaid's knees, too. 'Woman, if you take one more liberty—'

'The taxi cab who brought our luggage is coming back at seven-thirty,' she told him, unperturbed. She glanced at her watch. 'That's in ten minutes. He's bringing a heap of groceries—I gave him a list—including baby food, nappies—*and pizza!*'

'*Pizza!*' Not for nothing was Luke a giant on Wall Street. He focused on the important thing here straight away. 'Pizza's arriving here in ten minutes?'

'Wash first, then we eat,' she told him. 'I even found

soap. It looks handmade and it's gorgeous. There's a pile in the bathroom cupboard. And I've dusted off some towels. Dinner's outside by the fire in ten minutes, Mr Grey. Get yourself washed and you're welcome to join us.'

How could he resist an invitation like that?

Luke headed for the bathroom, which, even though the years had made their ravages here as well, still smelt strangely of his mother and his grandmother. He washed under the cold water—tomorrow he'd have to see what was happening with the hot water service—and then he stood for a long time staring in the dusty mirror at his face.

The last time he'd looked in this mirror he'd been so young. He'd come home from boarding school for the weekend and his grandmother had had a heart attack.

'Go wash up, boy,' a neighbour had told him, taking rough sympathy on his tear-streaked self. The ambulance had left, and the boy couldn't have stayed here alone. 'Get yourself ready and we'll take you back to school.'

And that was that. He'd stared for a long time into this mirror, knowing he'd been irretrievably changed: he was now alone. Then he'd walked out of the house, and he'd known in his gut that he wouldn't be back. That had been the end of his family. First his grandfather, then his mother, and finally Gran…

Loving people hurt. Getting attached hurt.

Coming back here hurt like hell!

'Oh, for heaven's sake, get out there and eat your pizza,' he told his older, wiser face. 'I don't know why on earth you're bothering with this kid—with a baby!—but if you must, you must. Just organise her a life and then get out. Take your car and ride off into the sunset. Fast.'

Because any other way would lead to…what? Emotional attachment? Pain he'd sworn never to experience again.

No. He couldn't face that.

And then he heard a horn sound at the gate, and a cow lowing in the distance as it was forced to move aside for the taxi. Here, then, was dinner. And nappies. And domesticity.

'It's just for a week,' he told himself harshly. 'And then you leave!'

CHAPTER THREE

DINNER was a very, very different affair to the way Luke usually enjoyed it. Dinner, for him, was usually a social event. Sure, he was accustomed to eating out, but his eating out included expensive restaurants and cordon bleu food and beautiful women...

Here there was no expensive decor, the food was certainly not cordon bleu and the women... There were three. Grace and Gabbie and Wendy. Three women, and each was so far from his usual company it almost made Luke smile.

'What?' said Wendy, as she saw him take his mouthful of pizza and stare down at it as if it was food landed from Mars. 'Don't you like it?'

He looked at it with doubt. Did he? Bay Beach Pizza was hardly gourmet fare. 'It's not even wood-fired,' he offered.

'Oh, sadness! Welcome to the real world.' Wendy grinned. 'Wood-fired pizza... Good grief! Wave it over the fire, and give it some smoke if you must. Me, I'm just going to eat mine!'

She did, and she enjoyed every mouthful. Well, why not? They were eating their pizza sitting on the edge of the veranda, with the camp fire they'd lit blazing brightly between them and the sea. It was a glorious night. The sun was setting behind the house, the breeze was warm and the sound of the surf was a series of hushed murmurs as it flowed in and out to the shore. The smell—of fragrant eucalyptus, of old wood burning slowly to embers, and of sea and salt and pizza—was good enough to bottle.

It was just great, Wendy thought. She sat back and watched as Gabbie seriously engaged in pizza-eating—everything was a serious business for Gabbie—and Luke fed his baby sister the bottle Wendy had prepared for him, and down in the paddocks the cows looked up in wonder.

'The cows think we're crazy,' she told Gabbie. 'Fancy eating pizza when we have all this great grass!'

Gabbie looked at her gravely—and then her small face crinkled into a smile. She gave a tentative chuckle. 'That's silly.'

'It is, isn't it?' She swept the little girl up into her arms and hugged, pizza and all. If she was any happier she'd burst. This could work! If Gabbie's mother kept away...

She looked over to Luke and found him watching her strangely. He was like the cows, she thought—he couldn't understand where she was coming from.

'Tell me about you,' he asked her softly. 'What made you become a Home mother? Why are you here?'

That was easy. 'I'm here because this is the best place in the world. Isn't it, Gabbie?'

'No, but—'

'But what?' She raised her eyebrows and it made him pause.

What indeed? She was an employee, he told himself. Just an employee. He shouldn't delve any deeper than he needed. But he hadn't had an employee like this before, and she had him fascinated.

'Tell me what your qualifications are, for a start.'

'You'll sack me if I don't make the grade?'

He sighed and shifted Grace to the other knee—and then looked down in dismay at the knee she'd been shifted from. It was wet! Heck, how many nappy changes did babies need?

'I'm not sacking you,' he told her, but he was now thoroughly distracted. 'Holy cow! Look at this. How can she be wet already? You realise I only have one pair of trousers? You might have luggage for a lifetime, but for me this was only meant to be a day trip.'

'More fool you,' she said serenely. 'Never take a baby anywhere without changes of clothes for everyone. It's the first rule of parenting, Mr Grey.'

'Then, it's lucky I don't need to learn any more,' he said tartly, and then caught himself as Grace looked up at him. His half-sister's tiny eyes widened—and it was as if she'd understood what he'd said and was gazing at him with reproach.

Hell! This wasn't just a baby, he thought suddenly. This was a *person!* She was a little girl who'd grow up and want to know her family. Who'd need to be told...

His chain of thought was suddenly overwhelming and, Wendy, looking across at him, saw panic flare in his eyes. And understood.

'Luke, let's take one day at a time,' she said softly. 'You were worrying about wet trousers. I doubt we need to go any deeper than that at the moment.'

'Until tomorrow...'

'Until tomorrow,' she agreed and smiled. 'By tomorrow those wet trousers might start being on the nose and you'll definitely have to move on. But for now—as social workers, we tell our clients when they're having some overwhelming crisis to just focus on the next few minutes. Then the next few hours. The days will take care of themselves. Survival first, Luke, and everything else will follow.'

'So...' panic faded in the face of her calmness '...you're advising me to have another piece of pizza?'

'I guess I am.' She smiled her enchanting smile that, for some reason, made his insides do strange things. Sitting on this veranda where he'd spent such great times as a kid, looking out over the sea, holding a baby in his arms and having this woman sitting beside him...

This was about as far from his international jet-setting life as it was possible to be. He'd taken his shoes off—they were Gucci, after all, and a man didn't scrub floors in Gucci footwear—and his bare feet were brushing the grass as he sat on the edge of the veranda. His laptop computer was locked in the car boot and his phone was silent.

There were only the emerging stars and the silence of this place he'd loved. How long since he'd experienced a night like this?

How long until he would again?

He'd leave as soon as he had this mess sorted out, he decided, but then... The thought came out of nowhere, like a gift. When he came back he could visit! Whenever he was in Australia he could drive down to the country and see his half-sister—and this woman and her Gabbie. They'd be waiting for him, like a family.

The prospect gave him a warm glow right in the middle of his solar plexus and he couldn't help a tiny, smug smile creeping across his face.

Brilliant. This was brilliant!

'How often do you think you'll come?' Wendy asked, and he snapped back into the present with a start. She was eyeing him curiously, and by the look on her face she knew exactly what he was thinking.

'I...'

'Grace will need someone to attach to,' Wendy said softly. 'If her mother really doesn't want her...then, like it or not, you'll be it.'

'I guess I don't mind.' He thought it through, still feeling self-satisfied with his arrangements. What problem would one baby be? Money was no hassle and he'd have his secretary buy her gifts. He'd send them to her often...

But then the thought came back to him of his father, and how much his father's treatment of him had hurt. His father, paying expensive school fees, sending him over-the-top gifts, with cards not written in his handwriting.

Never wanting to see him…

'It doesn't work,' Wendy said softly. 'You know it doesn't.'

'What?'

'Being a parent by proxy.'

'You'd know?'

'I know.' She sighed and hugged Gabbie closer. Of course she knew. Some of the warmth went out of the evening and she hauled herself back to practicalities. And responsibility. Of course. That was her role in life. Picking up responsibility where other people left off… 'Ready for bed, love?' she asked the little girl.

'In my new bed with the pretty quilt?' Gabbie asked.

'That's the one.'

'And you'll stay out here?'

'Yes. Luke and Grace and I will be just under your window. We'll stay out here for a while because it's so dusty in the house. But I'll sit on your bed with you until you go to sleep. Okay?'

'Yes,' Gabbie said definitely. 'You'll stay with me until I go to sleep and then you and Luke and Grace will stay outside my window with the fire and the cows.'

'That's right.'

'That's good,' Gabbie said definitely. 'That will be very good.'

Woman and child left. Luke was left with the remaining pizza and one soggy baby lazily drinking her bottle and gazing up at him with eyes that wondered.

And wondered and wondered.

Just like him.

That's good. That will be very, very good...
Good grief!

Grace was fast asleep by the time Wendy returned, and Luke wasn't far behind. He started as she touched him on the shoulder, and then, as he turned to find her smiling down at him, the sight gave him an unexpected jolt. She did have this mystical quality, he thought. It was as if she was the sudden embodiment of a vision he'd thought was only a dream.

But in truth, she was real. In one hand she had Grace's carry-cot and in the other she had a pile of baby clothes.

'We need warm water,' she told him. 'And a bucket.'

'Why?' He raised his brows. 'We hardly have dishes to wash.'

'No, but we have a baby to wash,' she told him. 'That baby has spent half the day in wet clothes. We bathe her now or you spend the next few days walking a bundle of misery because she has a rash on her bottom. Okay?'

'Yes, ma'am.'

There was nothing else to say.

Grace hardly woke.

Baths, obviously, were one of her favourite things. She opened her eyes in sleepy wonder as Wendy lowered her naked person into the bucket of warm water. Then she smiled her gracious approval, fluttered her tiny hands in the suds, and lay back in sleepy delight.

For some reason Luke couldn't take his eyes from her. This was his half-sister, he kept thinking. His sister. His...family?

He hadn't had family for so long, and now, suddenly, she was partly his—and she was just beautiful. By the time Wendy had finished soaping Grace's small pink body, Luke was near as not in love with her. What a sweetie!

His sister...

Afterwards, she lay on warm towels and Wendy expertly slipped her into dry clothes, and her eyes closed again before she was dressed. She snuggled into her carry-cot with a contented sigh, and fell instantly asleep.

God was in his heaven. All was right with Grace's small world, and Luke's world was still realigning itself on its axis—an axis that had somehow tilted...

'I can't believe her mother could just give her up,' Wendy said slowly, looking down at the sleeping baby, and there was such a look of pain on her face that Luke thought for a moment that he must have imagined it.

He hadn't. She turned away, but as she did he saw the glimmer of tears on her lashes. So, social worker or not, Wendy wasn't quite impervious to human drama.

'Tell me what your background is?' he asked her again as she bundled towels and baby clothes together.

She shook her head. 'I have things to do.'

'Yeah, right. Like running the washing machine—without electricity, without hot water and without a washing machine.' He patted the bare boards beside him, inviting her to sit. 'We have two sleeping children. It's grown-ups' time now.'

That made her smile. 'I guess, for you, it's always grown-ups' time.'

'I don't have a lot to do with children,' he agreed. 'Until now.'

'And now it's only for a week.'

'As you say...' He looked at her, his eyes asking a question. 'Go on, then.' He held out a hand, took hers and tugged, so she had to sink down to sit beside him. For some reason she was reluctant—but there was no good reason not to.

It was just, he made her feel...

Peculiar. She wasn't taking it any further than that, she decided, as she pulled her hand away. She couldn't afford to. If there was one thing Wendy Maher had decided all those years ago it was that men were trouble. And this one looked more trouble than most.

'I'll give you my résumé if you like,' she said, lowering herself to perch on the edge of the veranda and then staring out to the distant sea. Distancing herself... 'It's very good.'

'All this and modest to boot?'

'If I don't sing my praises no one will.' She smiled. 'I have a first-class honours degree in social work. I have nursing training—only one year but it's enough for what I need it for. I have five years' experience as a Home mother at Bay Beach Orphanage.'

He frowned at that. It didn't quite fit. 'I would have imagined a social worker with a first-class honours degree would have been working in an organisational capacity rather than hands-on child care,' he said thoughtfully. 'Surely you don't need those qualifications to be a Home mother.'

'I like children,' she said, and her voice was suddenly clipped.

'You always wanted to be a Home mother?'

'No. Only when...'

'Only when your husband died?'

'I...yes.'

'I see.' He nodded. 'So when you say if you don't sing your praises no one else will—it's because you're totally alone in the world?'

'I have friends.'

'Friends aren't the same,' he said softly. 'I figured out that one early.'

'When your mother died.'

'As you say.' He shrugged. 'My grandparents and my

mother died within two years of each other. It was pretty hard.'

'I'd imagine it must have been.' There was soft sympathy in her tone and he looked curiously across at her. She was sitting staring out into the moonlight, her face serene and calm. What she had said was an open invitation—to tell her all his troubles. Lay it all on her.

How many people had done that to her, he thought suddenly. Wendy was that sort of woman. It was an almost irresistible compulsion—to burden her with his needs...

Somehow he managed not to. 'You haven't finished telling me about you,' he told her, and he received a surprised look for his pains. He was right, then. She was a woman who took on other people's troubles and kept her own close to her heart.

'What else do you need to know?'

He surveyed her thoughtfully. What else...?

'How did your husband die?'

'Car crash,' she said briefly. 'How else?'

How else indeed? There was a story behind this. 'You sound bitter.'

'Do I?' She caught herself and managed a smile. 'I shouldn't be. It was a long time ago.'

'It was a good marriage?'

Her breath sucked in at that. He'd overstepped the mark and he knew it straight off. 'That, Mr Grey, is none of your business,' she told him. 'And there are better ways to be exercising your mind right now than by going over past history.'

He was still watching her—this lady with shadows. 'Like what?'

'Like, where are we going to sleep?' Ever practical, Wendy's mind closed completely to the nerve ends he'd just exposed. She'd learned long ago what to do when life slapped her in the face, or when something made her think of the past. She looked about her for what came next—and then she did it. Right now!

'Mattresses,' she said firmly, and he blinked.

'Pardon?'

'You can sleep in the house if you want,' she told him frankly. 'But I'm not. I'll sneeze all night. We have Gabbie's room habitable—just—but the rest of the house is an environmental nightmare. Air pollution two hundred and twenty per cent and rising, I'd guess. We've stirred up dust that hasn't been touched for twenty years. I'll sleep on a mattress out here, under Gabbie's window so I'll hear if she wakes.'

'Are you sure you don't want us to pick ourselves up and go to a hotel?' he said almost desperately, and she grinned.

'Where's your sense of adventure, Luke Grey? Sleeping outdoors is good for the soul. Two mattresses and a couple of the quilts I thumped the living daylight out of, and we're set for the night.'

'But—'

'Oh, for heaven's sake,' she said, exasperated. 'You've brought me here, Luke. You've shown us our new home, and we're here to stay.'

It was the strangest night.

They dragged mattresses outside and set them up with quilts. Wendy used the bathroom—cold water only—and then, when it was Luke's turn, he came out to find she was already under her quilt and ready for sleep. There was nothing for him to do but follow—under his own quilt on his own mattress four feet away.

It was so different!

Since ending university, Luke had been accustomed to

money. He'd studied commerce and law, and his brilliant mind meant he'd been employed before the ink was dry on his degrees. He'd moved straight into a world where money was counted in thousands—or millions—and he'd lived in five-star luxury ever since.

He'd almost forgotten his roots. He'd almost forgotten why his mother had fought for custody and fought to bring him back here. He'd forgotten there were things money couldn't buy. Like this place. The sea air. The silence.

Now he lay on his back on the mattress, with his hands linked behind him, and he stared upward at the veranda roof and saw the frayed ends of rope where a swing had once hung. A swing his mother had pushed him on, over and over.

Gabbie could have a swing like that, he thought—and after Gabbie, Grace.

'Tell me about Gabbie,' he said softly, into the hushed silence where the murmur of the sea was the only sound for ever. There was no traffic noise which felt truly strange. Luke hadn't slept without traffic noise for twenty years. There was only silence…and his companions. But he knew Wendy wasn't asleep and he badly wanted to talk.

'Gabbie doesn't look five years old,' he tried again softly. 'And…she looks scared.'

'Her story's not very pretty,' Wendy murmured into the dark, and he knew once more that she was considering him. Letting him off the hook if he didn't really want to hear.

Hell, did she never think of herself? Where were *Wendy's* needs in all this?

But she wouldn't talk of herself. He knew that now.

Focus on Gabbie…

'So what is her story?' he probed, and she sighed.

'If you really want to know.'

'If my plan works, she'll be growing up with my half-sister,' he growled. 'I need to know her background.'

In the dark he felt rather than saw her smile. 'I guess you do. Of course, you've been so desperate to obtain impeccable references for anyone coming near your sister...'

'Don't give me a hard time, woman,' he told her, and she chuckled. *Nice,* he thought. She had the best chuckle. Rich and low, and so warm it made you want to reach out and...

Stop it! he ordered himself as a jab of reality sank home. This woman was his employee! If he messed this up, he'd have to find someone else to act as Grace's nanny. First rule of thumb—you don't mix business with pleasure!

Or business with...sex?

'Just tell me about Gabbie,' he managed hastily, hauling his thoughts back to logic with a savage jolt, and then he listened to the silence and wondered whether she'd reply.

She didn't for a long, long moment. Finally she tossed back her quilt and rose. What was she wearing? he thought numbly as he watched her in the moonlight—some sort of soft nightgown that looked incredibly pretty? There were suddenly all sorts of undesirable thoughts racing in his brain, and none of them had anything to do with the subject he'd just brought up.

But Wendy was focused on Gabbie now. She crossed to the open window into the house and stood for a minute listening to the steady breathing of the child sleeping just under the sill.

Finally, satisfied that Gabbie was deeply asleep, she settled herself on her mattress under her quilt again, and still his unwanted sensual thoughts raced—and finally she answered his question.

'Gabbie's mother is a truly dreadful person,' she said gently, and she said the harsh words so softly that for a minute Luke thought he hadn't heard right. It wasn't the sort of description he'd expect from such a woman as Wendy. He blinked into the night, but it came again. The harshness... 'I've met a lot of sad people since I've started this job, and I've met kids who've been abused in all sorts of ways. Usually I can see reasons. I try and understand. But Gabbie's mother, Sonia...'

Her voice grew hard—implacable. 'If I could wave a magic wand and have Sonia disappear from the face of the earth, I'd wave it. I've never felt like that about any other person, and I hope I never feel like that again.'

'Yes?' Luke was staring again at the frayed ends of rope where his swing had swung, but he'd been jolted out of his thoughts of the past—and his thoughts of Wendy as a very desirable woman. Almost... 'You're going to tell me why?'

She sighed then, a long deep sigh that told Luke more than anything how much she'd struggled over this.

'Sonia's a money-grubbing, egocentric control freak,' she said. 'One of the other social workers knows her background—she knew her husband.' Her voice fell away.

Damn, she had to go on now. 'Can you tell me?' he prodded.

'I shouldn't.'

'If I'm spending any time here with the girls, then maybe I need to know,' he said softly and thought, hell, maybe this was emotional blackmail. Did he intend to spend any time here?

But Wendy considered this and seemed to find it acceptable.

'Gabbie's dad was an accountant,' she said. 'According to my sources, Howard Rolands was a nice enough man but he made a serious mistake when he married Sonia.'

'In what way?'

Wendy shrugged. 'Rumour is that she married him for

money and bled him dry. I only know for sure that the marriage lasted hardly any time at all. Then Howard left her. He took Gabbie with him and Sonia fought him every inch of the way.'

'Maybe that's understandable,' Luke said, frowning. 'It's unusual for a mother not to get custody.'

'Which is why she won it in the end,' Wendy said bitterly. 'Not because she wanted Gabbie. She took Gabbie back to hurt Howard and then, for the next two years she kept her as a tool to hurt him more. She refused access, she mistreated the child—never quite enough to lose access, you understand, but there are ways of hurting a child without actual physical abuse. We have a folder an inch thick of this poor man's submissions to see more of his daughter. Finally he had a breakdown—and then he suicided.'

'Hell,' Luke said faintly into the night and Wendy nodded into the dark.

'That's right. It was hell. Only then, you see, Sonia didn't have anything to gain by keeping Gabbie. She had no one to hurt. So she dumped her on us, and signed the release papers for pre-adoption. I had her first when she was three years old—a tiny, damaged, waif-like child who was afraid to open her mouth.'

'And you fell for her?'

'I fall for a lot of my kids,' Wendy said ruefully. 'It's an occupational hazard. But Gabbie was special. I loved her and she blossomed, and then, when we figured she was ready for permanent bonding, we asked Sonia to sign the final adoption papers.'

'And...'

'Sonia's answer was to take her away from us. She did a really good line in devoted-mother-making-good and took her back.'

'But why?'

'Who'd know?' Wendy's voice was harsh in the moon-light. 'Certainly not because she loves her. She kept her for two months, undid all the good we'd done and then dumped her again. That time I was lucky enough to have a place free in the Home I was working in, so I took Gabbie back in with me. And it started all over again. Teaching her to trust. Preparing her for long-term bonding. And then Sonia moving in again to destroy all the good we'd achieved.'

'But—'

But Wendy wasn't listening to interruptions. It was as if she was talking to herself in the dark. 'Gabbie's been taken back six or seven times now, and after each time I've moved heaven and earth to get her back with me. The time before this I didn't manage it. The Home I was running was full, and she had to go somewhere else. She's starting to be permanently damaged, and I couldn't bear it so—'

'So you've quit your job over it?'

'Sonia doesn't really want her,' Wendy said wearily. 'I know that now. I've met the woman—done everything I can think of to make things right between them—but Sonia's only interest seems to be preventing anyone else making life good for Gabbie. She signs her over and over again for pre-adoption, but each time she backs out. It's as if she can't punish her husband any more so she'll punish Gabbie. Once Gabbie's with social welfare, Sonia doesn't even enquire where she is—until the next application comes up to have her permanently placed.' She sighed. 'But this way...'

'This way?'

'We've agreed that social services will leave her with me,' she said. 'I won't apply for adoption—we'll just quietly go on with our lives and hope Sonia leaves us alone. If she does interfere and takes Gabbie back, then, with social services' permission, I'll be waiting whenever she returns. Gabbie will know that. I'll always be here for her.'

Silence. Luke thought this over, mulling it into the night. And he didn't like what he thought.

'I think,' he said slowly, 'that that's the way of madness. To love a child and to let her go to someone like that, over and over... You'll tear your heart in two.'

'If I don't do this, then no one else will,' Wendy told him. 'I'm the only chance Gabbie has. Gabbie's mother might do her worst, but I need to be here, as a permanent refuge. I have to give her that chance.'

'As you'll give Grace a chance?'

'That's different.' Wendy smiled and Luke heard the smile in her voice. It was strange the way he was starting to know what her face would be doing, even though he couldn't see her. 'That's a paying proposition.'

'So you think you won't love my little half-sister like you love Gabbie?'

'In your dreams.' Wendy sounded startled. 'Payment or not, I'll love her to bits.'

'Now, how did I know you'd say that?' Luke grinned to himself. 'Loving people to bits. That's your speciality, isn't it, Wendy Maher?'

'Only children,' she said hastily.

'You'd never think of marrying again?' He got that in before he could help himself, and afterwards he could never figure out why he'd suddenly needed to know. Why her answer seemed so important...

To his surprise, she didn't back off, but answered him with another question. 'Why on earth would I want to do that?'

'It must get pretty lonely,' he said softly. 'Just with the kids.'

'Lonely like you are?' He heard her smile again. 'You don't have kids, Luke Grey, and you're not all that lonely—

as far as I can see. Mind, you have a wonderful car, don't you? Money on wheels. That's what love's all about, now, isn't it, Luke? A heap of metal on four bits of rubber and a man's smitten.'

And that was it. It was all he was going to get from her. She'd had enough questions for one night. She tried to take the faint note of bitterness from her voice as she turned away from him and pulled her quilt firmly around her, in a gesture that might almost have been defence.

'Goodnight, Luke,' she said gently, and she was nearly back on an even keel again. 'I have my kids and you have your car. Who could ask for more?'

Who indeed? His gorgeous car...

Luke tried to think of his car as he hauled his quilt up to his nose and tried to sleep himself. Wendy was right—or she had been until now. Thinking of his sleek little Aston Martin was usually the way he made his mind turn off tricky problems—financial dealings or love-life complexities. His car was an extravagance, he conceded, but she was worth every cent of what he'd paid for her. A man could lie in bed at night and know he'd made it when he owned that car.

But not tonight. Not now. Not with Wendy sleeping four feet from him, a tiny baby sleeping between them and one needful little girl just through the wall. His priorities seemed to have shifted.

He lay in bed and he couldn't keep his mind on his car for more than two seconds flat.

A man might have made it—but in Wendy's eyes he hadn't made it anywhere, Luke thought bitterly.

Nowhere at all.

When he woke she was feeding his baby.

The veranda was facing east. The sun rising over the sea

was basking them in the glow of dawn, and his first sight was Wendy sitting on the edge of the veranda with Grace in her arms.

He could only stare.

She was wearing the same nightgown she'd been wearing the night before. By moonlight it had looked soft and clingy and incredibly expensive—the sort of nightgown a man just had to touch. By daylight he saw it was not the least bit expensive—it was simple cotton and worn to softness rather than made that way—but it looked no less desirable. Wendy's hair had been untied from its knot—it was tumbling about her shoulders in a mass of dark, unruly curls—and the way she looked it wasn't her nightgown that looked soft and desirable. It was Wendy!

She was incredibly, gut-wrenchingly beautiful!

Why hadn't he seen that yesterday? Or...maybe he had, but every time he saw her she was growing more so.

'Good morning, Luke.' She turned and smiled at him, and her smile was enough to blast him back into oblivion. Her smile was dawn all on its own. 'I'm glad you've decided to rejoin the land of the living. I thought Grace would have woken everyone from here to Bay Beach, but you and Gabbie are obviously made of sterner stuff.'

'She...' His voice came out a sort of squeak and he coughed and tried again. For heaven's sake—there was something about this woman that made him feel as if he was a fifteen-year-old adolescent with his first crush. Now he was sounding like it! He deliberately lowered his voice. 'She was crying?' It came out as a ridiculous growl, and her eyes creased into laughter.

'Yes, Luke, she was crying. Yelling, more like. She's a lady who knows what she wants. I imagine it must be a family trait.'

That set him back. Family traits...

He had family! he thought again suddenly, with a jolt of awareness that made him blink. Right here, in this gorgeous woman's arms, was his family.

This was feeling better and better by the minute.

'Can I suggest you get up and stoke our fire?' she said, bursting his euphoric bubble. 'I had trouble heaping enough embers to heat Grace's bottle, and we'll need more for breakfast.'

'Breakfast?' He glanced at his wristwatch. 'It's only six,' he said weakly. He'd lain awake and thought for a large part of the night, and a man could do with more sleep now. 'Maybe after she's had her bottle we might go back to bed for a bit.'

'In your dreams.' Her smile widened. 'Try explaining to a five-month-old baby that it's not morning. Grace has practically slept around the clock, and you can't ask more than that.'

He guessed he couldn't. Grimacing he pushed his quilt back, and then wished he hadn't done that as well.

He'd brought no clothes with him—certainly no pyjamas. He'd hauled off his trousers and shirt the night before and what was left was what she now saw. All he had on was a pair of silk boxer shorts, deep black and emblazoned with tiny red hearts. They were a Valentine's gift from one of the ladies in his New York office. He'd forgotten he was wearing them—until now.

Wendy's eyes widened at the sight. They sparkled mischievously and he hauled up his quilt as if he was about to be shot and his quilt was his only defence.

'Hey, don't mind me.' She chuckled. 'You're seeing me in my nightie. I don't mind seeing you in your PJs.'

'I do not usually wear heart-emblazoned boxer shorts to bed,' he said sourly, and her grin widened.

'No. Of course not. They're day wear. I can see that.'

'Wendy!'

'Mmm?'

'Will you remember I'm your employer,' he told her, trying for severity. 'I'd like a bit of respect.'

'And you have it.' She schooled her grin into manageable proportions. 'Who could not respect a man who wears boxers like that to work every day?'

Right. He glared.

'Firewood, then,' she said demurely, and turned her back on him, taking pity on him enough to allow him to dress himself with a semblance of dignity.

But he knew that she was still laughing inside.

CHAPTER FOUR

'THE priorities, as I see it, are these.'

Luke blinked. That was the sort of line he was accustomed to tossing around at board meetings and the like. He wasn't accustomed to having it tossed at him, especially by a woman who looked as if she'd come off a communal hippie farm, and who had her arms full of children.

They'd had their breakfast—sort of. On inspection, the crockery cupboard in the kitchen had been taken over by mice and Wendy declared she wasn't touching anything without disinfecting first. Therefore they'd given cereal a miss and eaten bread toasted by holding it on a stick over the fire and buttered in their hands, and they'd drunk milk straight from the cartons the taxi driver had brought the night before. Curiously, it was delicious.

'It's like a breakfast picnic,' Gabbie had declared gamely, from her safe position right behind Wendy's skirts, and Luke had been inclined to agree with her.

'First priority, hot water?' he suggested, trying to regain the initiative, but Wendy nodded and the initiative was still with her.

'I checked it last night. The hot water runs through the fire stove so that's your first job. The chimney needs cleaning.' She glanced at her watch. 'As soon as it's decent you can ring an electrician and a glazier and the telephone company. That will get our urgent services seen to. If you pay enough we'll get immediate help but a chimneysweep will take weeks. There's no one local. Therefore...' she gave him a sympathetic smile '...it's you.'

Luke groaned. 'No.'

'There should be nothing to it.' She chuckled. 'We can do it like the bad old days if you like—I'll pretend I'm the worst kind of chimneysweep, we poke you up and then we light a fire beneath you. That way we get a really clean chimney fast.'

'Or me roasted for lunch. Thanks very much.' He groaned again. 'Am I to spend the week scrubbing?' He looked down at his already filthy clothes. 'I need to get myself some gear.'

'You do at that,' she agreed. Her eyes grew thoughtful, and he could see she was tossing over options. 'I think, after you organise me some electricity, some chopped wood and a clean chimney, I might give you leave of absence for a bit.'

'Gee, thanks.'

She wasn't finished yet. 'You need to do something urgently about Grace,' she added, and he frowned.

'Like what?'

'Like getting yourself some legal protection,' she told him. 'I've been thinking. The way things are, if Grace's mother turned up she could accuse you of all sorts of things—kidnapping included—and it's your word against hers.'

He was startled. 'She wouldn't do that. She dumped her on me.'

'People do all sorts of strange things,' Wendy said softly, hugging Gabbie close. She had Grace in her other arm, and with her two littlies cradled against her she looked like a protective mother hen.

She was used to fighting for kids, Luke thought suddenly—and he also thought there was no one he'd rather have on his side. She was some woman!

Somehow he dragged his thoughts back to practicalities. To Grace's mother…

'Why on earth would she accuse me of kidnapping Grace?'

'If Lindy is angry at how your father treated her, there's nothing to say she won't take that anger out on you.'

'She wouldn't—'

'Maybe she wouldn't,' Wendy said soothingly. 'But you need to cover yourself. Find her, get yourself a lawyer and have him witness her agreement that you're taking care of her child. The sooner you do it, the better.'

He thought that over, the memory of Wendy's description of Sonia ringing in his ears. Hell…

'Maybe I'd best go straight away.'

'No.'

'No?'

'Not quite. You have a chimney to clean,' she told him. 'And there's something else.'

'Yes?'

'I've told you,' she went on calmly, as though it was a tiny detail she was just adding, 'I have no protection either. If you leave, then I have no legal right to care for Grace.'

'I'll cover you,' he said quickly. 'If there's any problem then I'll protect you. And I should be back in a couple of days.'

'That's the trouble,' she told him, her eyes cool and unchallenging. 'People don't come back. If there's one thing I've learned in this job, it's that.'

His brows snapped together in anger. 'You don't trust me?'

She was unperturbed by his anger. 'I trust no one when a child's future is at stake,' she told him. 'On their behalf, I can't afford to.'

'But—'

'But don't worry.' She smiled again and there was now a hint of mischief lurking deep in her eyes. 'I've been figuring out surety and I know what you can leave behind so I know you'll come back.'

'What?' But somehow he suspected what was coming before she said it. His heart sank as her smile deepened. Oh, no!

And here it was, right on cue. 'Your car,' she said sweetly.

Okay, he'd suspected it, but it didn't mean he was ready and waiting. He blenched as Gabbie looked at him with eyes that didn't trust him an inch and Wendy watched him with eyes that asked just how serious he was about taking care of his baby sister.

'My car,' he said finally, knowing he was beaten before he even started.

'That's right.' She smiled again. 'As I said, I've been thinking things over. I can't stay here without transport. What if one of the children was to become ill, or there was an accident? Plus there's the shopping and I can't use taxis all the time. You must see I need to be able to go back and forth to Bay Beach. I know that as a concerned employer you'll be providing me with a car before you leave for good.'

'But—'

'But meanwhile we can kill two birds with one stone,' she interrupted blithely. 'You can phone a hire firm from Bay Beach and have them rent you wheels of some kind. Then you can leave your Noddy car here for us.'

'My *Noddy* car!'

'Your Noddy car.' She chuckled at the look on his face. 'We like it, don't we, Gabbie? We'd prefer it in canary yellow, but we're prepared to overlook that one small blemish. This way we'll have something to do the grocery shopping in.'

'You'll use *my car* to do the supermarket shopping?' He was practically gibbering.

'And then we know you'll come back,' she ended serenely. 'That is—if you still want Gabbie and me to look after your baby?'

She raised her eyebrows and waited. He glared at her and she smiled straight back.

'What sort of a bargain is this?' His voice was practically rising through the roof. 'My *car*...'

'It's a baby bargain,' she told him, and her smile slipped a little. 'And you don't need to panic. We'll take the very best care of your precious car, and you know we'll take the very best care of your precious baby, too. That's what this is all about, isn't it?' She tilted her head and watched his face. 'A baby. Not a car?'

'I don't have a choice,' he said bitterly.

'I'm afraid you don't.' Surprisingly her voice held a trace of sympathy, and her hand came out to touch his. It was as if she really did understand what his car meant to him. Her touch was strong and warm and somehow...somehow it made a difference. 'You don't have a choice,' she agreed. 'But that's life. It's full of really, really tough breaks—like having to use a hire car for a couple of days. Now, Mr Grey...' laughter returned '...about that chimney...'

What on earth was he getting into? Luke reluctantly tackled the fire stove but his mind was only about ten per cent on the job. The rest was figuring out how much his life had changed in twenty-four hours, and why he'd let himself be talked into leaving his precious Aston Martin with a woman and two children...

When he went overseas he left his car in a special garage,

carefully enfolded in a climate-controlled autobag. Here, the garage behind the house was tumbling down and unfit for use. There was no safe place here to leave it. His pride and joy would have to stay parked outside in the sea air—and there were crows and parrots and even seagulls...

'There must be a bird's nest blocking the chimney.' Wendy's voice came from behind him and he jumped a foot. He hit his head on the mantelpiece and swore.

'Hey, hush.' Wendy clapped her hands over Gabbie's ears—the little girl was never more than two inches away from her—and she fixed Luke with a school-marm look. She appeared not to even notice that he was rubbing his head in pain! 'Gabbie doesn't know words like that—do you, Gabbie?'

Gabbie chuckled and sank back against Wendy's skirt. When she smiled, her elfin face lit up like a sunbeam and Luke found his heart twisting. Just a little, mind, not too much—not so much as you'd write home about—at the treatment that had been meted out to this child.

Good grief! he thought, as he stared at the pair of them. He wasn't a soft touch. He didn't like children! So what was happening here? The emotion he was feeling was building all the time, and he had to stay impartial. He was simply setting up a home for his little sister because it was expected of him, he told himself—and then he was getting out of here.

But Wendy was still concentrating on chimneys. 'If you stick your nose up the chimney you can't see daylight,' Wendy said wisely. 'I tried it last night. It took me ages to open the damper but when I did it was still black. There must be a bird's nest blocking the top.'

'I don't wish to stick my nose up the chimney,' Luke snapped, thrown totally off balance. 'You have your belongings here, lady. I don't even have a change of clothes.'

'You'll be able to buy something in Bay Beach on the way back to Sydney,' she said kindly. 'After all, what's another suit of clothes to a wealthy young futures broker like you?'

'Oh, right.' He glared. 'So I just meander into Bay Beach Menswear, wearing soot up to my armpits!'

'It was just a suggestion,' she said hastily. 'If you're going to be crabby—'

'I am *not* crabby.'

'Let's go, Gabbie.' Wendy pulled Gabbie backwards out the door, her eyes still brimming with laughter. 'We'll leave Uncle Luke to his chimney sweeping—without nose-poking. Though how he's going to do it and stay clean...'

'So what are *you* doing?' he yelled after her, exasperated.

'Women's work,' she yelled back cheerfully. 'Gabbie and I are going to address the issue of a bag of soiled nappies.' He heard the laughter in her voice. 'Want to swap jobs, Mr Grey?'

'No, thank you,' he said hastily—and stuck his nose up the chimney, soot and all.

Handyman was hardly a description that fitted Luke well. By the time he'd been old enough to learn any useful skills in that direction, he'd been sent to boarding school. Since then there'd always been a janitor or a maintenance man or a gardener to take care of any crisis.

There wasn't one on call now, and he needed one badly.

Wendy was right. The view, through the two-inch-wide crack available after wedging open the damper, was of unmitigated blackness.

Sighing deeply, he headed for the garage to see if he could find a ladder.

'Giving up already?' Wendy called. Grace was rolling happily on a rug on the cattle-cropped grass below the veranda, and Wendy and Gabbie were plunging things that

Luke didn't want to know about into buckets of water. It was an incredibly domestic scene, and, imperceptibly, his mood changed. His chest expanded a mite and he rolled up his sleeves. These might well be *his* kids and *his* woman— and he was doing man's work.

'There's a ladder under the house,' she told him, and his bubble pricked a bit at her look of concern. 'If that's what you're looking for. But you be careful on the roof.'

'I have it under control,' he told her, setting his chin, caveman-like—off to hunt his dinosaur for lunch. 'You just stick to your business and I'll stick to mine.'

His chauvinism didn't last. *She* was concerned. How about him?

Luke balanced on the ladder—he'd used it to climb onto the roof and had hauled it up after him to balance it against the chimney. Now, with his feet feeling decidedly insecure beneath him, he stared down into the abyss.

There was a bird's nest in the chimney. How they'd managed to build it there he didn't know, but it was a vast, untidy conglomeration of sticks, wedged about two feet down.

At least there weren't any eggs or baby birds in sight, he thought, thanking heaven for small mercies. He didn't have to make any life or death decisions here. It must be an old nest.

'What's the problem?'

Luke looked down—and then wished he hadn't. Wendy was a long, long way down, standing on the grass by Grace and staring up at him anxiously.

'There isn't one.' Heck, a man had some pride. He took a deep breath and then managed to raise the rake he'd hauled up here over his head. 'It's a bird's nest. I'll dislodge it.'

He looked upward—much better than downward—at the circle of irate crows fussing over his head. The birds had been squawking from the moment he'd put his foot on the first step of the ladder—defending their territory.

'I'd guess it's either us or the crows, so there's no choice,' he called to Wendy. 'A man has to do what a man has to do.' He positioned his rake.

'Luke…'

'If I hook it I'll be able to pull it up.'

'I don't think so—'

No. Suddenly neither did he. The rake caught the edge of the nest and, once one side was dislodged, the entire thing caved in and plummeted down to rest on the damper below.

'Yuck.' Wendy was as covered in soot as he was. They were back in the kitchen, hauling bits of nest out from the slit between damper and chimney. It was foul work, and it took for ever. 'This is disgusting, and any minute now I'm expecting to grab something that moves,' she said. 'Are you sure there were no baby birds up there?'

'Do I look like I'm the sort of man to empty babies from their nests?' he demanded, affronted. 'After all the work I've done in the interest of babies…'

'The crows up there looked worried.'

'I am *not* worried about worried crows.' He hauled a stick sideways through the crack, it resisted and then came with a rush of soot. Gabbie squealed as a shower of blackness coated all of them. 'Good grief.'

'They're making such a fuss!'

'There were *not* any birds in that chimney,' Luke confirmed. 'Just ancient nesting material.'

'It was the birdies' home,' Gabbie said solemnly.

'They can relocate.' Luke glowered. 'Just as long as it

isn't into the front seat of my car. Don't you dare leave the top down while...'

He didn't finish the sentence.

There was a terrified squawk from the inside of the chimney, a rush of scrambling wings and claws, and a cloud of soot bigger than all the rest showered over them.

What the...?

The squawking didn't stop. It grew louder and louder as, inside the chimney, a bird descended as if it was heading into the room.

The bird didn't come into the kitchen but it wasn't for want of trying. It couldn't. The damper stopped it in its tracks, just above the stove.

'It must be a young one that's just left the nest.' Wendy was sitting back on her heels, staring in horror at the feathers and soot fluttering through to the hearth. The noise was deafening and she had to practically shout to make herself heard. The trapped bird squawked as if there was no tomorrow and, above the roof, every crow from a ten-mile radius had come to lend a hand. Or wing. Or whatever.

'How do you know?' Luke's heart was sinking. Of all the stupid things. Now what? Gabbie's normally pale face was turning ashen. The child was expecting the worst, and Luke was starting to feel the same.

'If it's just left the nest then it would have flown back in without realising there was a problem,' Wendy told him. 'But instead of a platform of twigs, it's found thin air. It's fallen right down.' She stared at the fireplace as if it could give her some clue. 'Do you think...? Will it be able to claw its way back up?'

'No.' They'd been listening to the creature struggle for five minutes now, and the more it struggled the more hopeless its position became.

'Can we get the damper out?' Wendy whispered, and

Luke had to bend forward to hear. 'It seems firmly wedged.'

It was. Luke remembered the arrival of the damper. Twenty-five years ago, fed up with a kitchen full of blow-flies, his grandmother had arranged a man to fix it. It had taken the fix-it man two days to set the damper into place and secure it firmly with concrete.

Luke braved another look now, got a face full of soot for his pains and had his opinion confirmed. 'It'll take me hours—if not days—to get rid of the damper and I'd need special tools to do it,' he said slowly. Heaven knew what tools, but he had to say something. 'The bird would be dead by the time I got it out.'

'The birdy's going to die,' Gabbie sobbed, and Luke grimaced.

'It'll never come though the damper,' Wendy said. 'It won't fit.' Every now and then a leg or a wing appeared in their line of gaze, but the two-inch-wide slit would never allow a crow to squeeze through into the room. 'Do you think…? Could we somehow lasso it from the top and pull it up? There's rope under the house.'

'Yeah, right. My lassoing skills aren't what they should be. How about yours?'

'Luke…' Wendy closed her eyes, despair rising. 'I guess—'

'You guess what?'

She guessed nothing while Gabbie was listening. 'Honey, can you pop out to the veranda and make sure Grace is still okay?' Wendy said, and gave the child a gentle push doorwards. Gabbie went, but at the doorway she stopped and looked back.

'You'll save the birdy?' she asked, and her troubled eyes were directed straight at Luke.

What was a man to do with a look like that?

'I'll do my best,' he said, but something in the way he said it must have worked, because her look settled and became one of trust.

'Uncle Luke will get you out,' she called to the bird, and then walked out, the door swinging closed behind her.

She left them to silence. Apart from crow noises—which meant there wasn't any silence at all. It just felt like silence because neither of them could think of a thing they could say.

'We'll have to put it out of its misery.'

'Sorry?' Luke was staring uselessly at the fireplace, his mind heading off on one tangent after another, all of no use whatsoever. Then he realised what she'd just said. He blenched. Kill it? No! 'For heaven's sake...'

'Well, think of another idea, then,' she snapped. 'I'm not leaving the creature to suffer for days while it slowly starves to death—and we can't dismantle the chimney. Can we?'

That was a bit much.

'Well, think of *something*. You pushed the stupid nest down.'

'Wendy—'

'*Do* something!' It was too much for Wendy. Birds trapped in chimneys were apparently not enclosed in her folio of crises-to-stay-calm-in.

Do something. But what? What?

Maybe... Luke found himself watching the crow's feet appearing and disappearing. As the creature struggled, its claws sank below the damper. They disappeared as it hauled itself up again, but after a while they appeared again. The crow couldn't always hold its claws above the level of the damper, so...

So maybe....

'Did you say we have a rope?' he demanded.

Something in his voice got through, and Wendy's face changed. She took a deep breath and fought for calm. 'Yes. I saw one under the house with the ladder.'

'If I could attach it to the claws...'

'And pull it out?' Once again she veered into panic. 'It won't fit through the damper no matter how hard you pull. You must see that. Luke, don't be stupid. It'd be squashed as you pulled it out, and I so much don't want it dead.'

'Neither do I,' he said, still frowning. Wendy's face was white, and suddenly it wasn't just the crow's fate at stake here. 'I don't know whether I can do this, Wendy, but let me try.'

'What?'

'Just go and get me the rope. Please. And let me think.'

He needed gloves.

Crows' claws were ripping instruments of destruction. To catch them he needed to protect his hands.

While Wendy searched for rope, he went on a fast tour of the house. The blankets he found were thin and would shred. The quilts were thicker, but they were handmade and gorgeous. They'd rip and he wouldn't sacrifice them.

What then? The carpets? No. They were far too thick and unwieldy.

Surely his grandmother had had gardening gloves. Somewhere...

She hadn't. Sigh. Wendy's face stayed with him, white and fearful. Hell! He didn't feel like hero material, but if he was all that was available...

There was only one thing to be done, and he didn't like it one bit. If he'd known, then the Italian designer would have had kittens, but it seemed he had no choice. To sacrifice all for one bird...

So when Wendy returned to the kitchen he was kneeling before the stove, ready and waiting. She stopped and stared at the sight that met her in stunned amazement. Luke had tied knots in the cuffs of his jacket, and he had his hands in the leather sleeves, testing how much flexibility he had in his fingers.

His gorgeous leather jacket... She handed him the rope in stunned silence.

'Luke, your jacket...'

'It's nothing.' It wasn't nothing at all—he loved it—but the thought of Gabbie's face was haunting. And Wendy's. Maybe especially Wendy's. If he could get the damned bird out of the chimney without killing it, then maybe it'd be worth the sacrifice.

'Luke...'

'Let's just see if it works.' He gave her a reassuring grin and then tried his first plan of attack. With his hands safely encased in leather, he reached forward and caught a claw as it plunged forward. The crow gave a terrified squawk, but the leather protected his hands and he held the claw for long enough to know that he could do so again.

Great! There was no point in holding it for longer—yet— and he didn't. Released, the crow clattered its way a few inches up the chimney and then fell to the damper again, defeated.

But Luke wasn't. Far from it. Silently he lifted Wendy's rope and tested it by twisting it around his fingers. It was old and soft, and not too thick. Great! With luck, this could just work. Then, without saying a word, he headed outside. Wendy was left to follow.

Which she did, her face a picture of confusion.

'Just watch,' he told her. 'This might not work, but it's our best shot.'

So Gabbie and Wendy stood hand in hand, uncomprehending, while Luke climbed again onto the roof. Once more he hauled his ladder up after him. He tied one end of the rope to the ancient television aerial, and then he climbed to the chimney top with the other rope end in his hand.

And now there were maybe thirty crows whirling over his head, all squawking their distress at the top of their lungs. This was all he needed. It was so hard to keep his balance...

'If one more of you goes down this chimney then I'll find me a gun,' Luke said direfully, shaking a futile fist in the crows' direction. 'I'm giving you guys the benefit of the doubt and assuming the chap below is the family idiot. So learn a lesson from him.' He glared at them all—they were barely eighteen inches above him!—and then he lowered the end of the rope carefully down the chimney.

Below, Wendy still watched while Gabbie clung to her side and stared as well. The knowledge that they were there drove him on.

The rope descended. That was the first part of the task achieved. With the top of the rope still tied to the aerial, he climbed back down again to where Wendy and Gabbie were waiting.

'Do you mind telling me what you're doing?' Wendy's face was a bewildered picture and he almost grinned. It wasn't bad to have her on the unsettled side for once. For him to have the initiative. He squared his shoulders and headed for the veranda.

'Just hush and see if it works.' He gave Gabbie another reassuring grin, and ruffled her hair. 'So far so good. Our baby crow might rejoin its mother yet.'

'Luke...'

'Hush.'

Without any more explanation, he led them back to the kitchen. What a relief. Lying on the stove was the frayed end of the rope he'd just lowered. So far, so good—and his women's admiration didn't feel too bad either.

Then, with his hands in his leather sleeves to protect himself from the wildly slashing claws, and after one deep breath and a silent prayer—*please let this work*—he seized a claw.

The other claw slashed wildly downward—without the leather he'd be cut to bits—but now Luke was in resolution mode. This was a case of now or never, and it had to be now. Working like lightning, he tied the first claw with the rope and held on to it. He waited until the other claw came sweeping down again to slash—not more than two seconds—and somehow caught it and tied it together with the other leg.

Now he had two claws tied together with rope. Crossing his fingers, he released the trussed crow to thrash about in its chimney prison.

'I need to go back on the roof again,' he told his open-mouthed audience. 'And cross your fingers for me.'

'I'm even crossing my eyeballs,' Wendy said, stunned to her socks. 'You too, Gabbie. Cross everything.'

The little girl was too boggled to say a word.

Finally, up on the roof again, the whole process started to come together. Standing on his ladder against the chimney, carefully, inch by inch Luke manoeuvred the rope upward.

For the first few seconds he thought the crow would never come—it went wild as its feet were hauled slowly upward. But then, unbelievably, it seemed to relax a little. Its wings flapped but not with its previous power. Maybe it was starting to exhaust itself. Or maybe…maybe it sensed this was its only chance.

It rose and rose, and the whole world seemed to hold its breath. Luke pulled and pulled. He was standing alone, but strangely he didn't feel alone. Wendy was with him every inch of the way, and so was Gabbie. Even Grace…

Two feet from the top came the tricky part. Sensing freedom, the crow surged upward, lunging joyously into daylight. But still it was tied, and it was all Luke could do to regain his hold on the ladder. Somehow, and he could never afterwards figure out how, he managed to climb down to the roof with the crow flapping like a crazy, living kite in his hands.

There, with his arms still in his leather coat, and propped against the chimney to balance himself, he reeled the bird in toward him. With a faster action than he believed possible, and maybe a bit of luck as well, he got the claws untied. The crow flapped backwards and fell awkwardly onto the roof.

Was it hurt?

Not too badly, Luke thought incredulously as he watched it. Not so you'd notice. With a final squawk of indignant freedom, the bird rose skyward. It soared, was welcomed into the circle of waiting birds—and together they surged away, croaking harsh cries of jubilation as they went.

Luke was left sitting on the roof, an empty rope and a ruined leather jacket in his hands. He had the biggest grin on his face!

And his audience had seen everything.

'You've done it! Oh, come down, come down...' Down below, Wendy was laughing and crying all at the same time. She'd picked up Gabbie and the two of them were doing a crazy dance of triumph on the grass. 'Come on down, Luke Grey. You wonderful, wonderful man!'

He got down as fast as he could. Wendy and Gabbie were holding the ladder and, as he hit ground, he was enfolded in triumphant arms.

'Oh, Luke, that was so good.' Wendy was crying openly now, but laughing through her tears, and Gabbie couldn't stop smiling. Wendy was holding the little girl in her arms but suddenly he was in there too, the little girl sandwiched between them.

He'd hardly grown accustomed to the fact that he was being hugged—hugged, for heaven's sake!—when Wendy let him go, thrusting the little girl forward so he was holding Gabbie in his arms. But she'd only left to retrieve Grace from her blanket—and to envelop the baby in their sandwich squeeze as well. She was practically war-whooping.

'Luke, that was the most marvellous…the most marvellous…'

It was too much. Through kids and laughter and tears she somehow reached forward and kissed him.

And in that kiss, something changed for ever.

To stand on the front lawn of a place he'd once loved, with his arms full of kids, with the squawking birds above them, and holding a woman who was weeping with joy…

Kissing a beautiful woman…

She started it, he would tell himself later, trying to figure out how it had happened. She kissed him, leaning forward so her lips touched his. But it suddenly wasn't Wendy doing the kissing. His arms were full of a tangle of children, but he had long arms and he could enfold them all.

Gabbie and Baby Grace were somehow in the middle but his mouth was on Wendy's, her lips were full and warm and loving—and she felt like no other woman he'd kissed in his life before. He felt his insides stir and shift, and his life somehow refocused, right at that point. Things became clear that had been clouded, and things that had been important suddenly took a step back.

Something huge was changing here. Why?

He didn't know. All he understood was that—well, she tasted of soot, she smelt of baby powder and milk formula, and she felt like…

She felt like heaven!

His hold grew tighter. He didn't understand what was happening to him—to them both!—but he wasn't letting go for a minute. Wendy...

His need was growing more urgent by the minute, but it couldn't last. Not like this.

'Hey, I'm squashed.' From somewhere below kiss level, Gabbie didn't sound in the least distressed—she sounded as if she was giggling—but it was enough to haul him somehow to his senses. It allowed him space to back away and look down into Wendy's emotion-filled face—and see the confusion he was feeling mirrored there threefold.

'The birdy's safe,' Gabbie squeaked, in a squashed but awed and delighted voice. 'We saved the birdy.'

'Yes, Gabbie, we did just that.' He was still watching Wendy, but with a wrench, it seemed, she'd hauled her attention to the children. She gave him one, single, startled glance and took Gabbie from him, handing him Grace. She then backed and stooped to set Gabbie on her feet. She turned her attention deliberately to the little girl, leaving him still holding Grace—but he was watching Wendy's colour turn blush-pink under her tan.

And he still didn't understand what was happening. All he knew was that something was—and it was something big. Huge!

'It flew away with its mummy and daddy,' Gabbie said proudly.

'It did.' Luke was finding it hard to make his voice work. What was going on here? He'd kissed other women—lots—and it had never felt like this.

'And its brothers and sisters were waiting for it.' Gabbie was practically glowing with pride. 'We saved its life.'

'And you held the ladder,' Luke told her, somehow recovering. Or recovering a little. 'I never could have managed if you hadn't held the ladder.'

'Really?' The little girl was close to bursting with pleasure.

'Really.'

'Well...' Gabbie sighed, then tucked her chin down into her chest with a look that Luke was starting to recognise. This was a child who internalised her pleasure—she wasn't brave enough to share in case it was snatched from her. Then she seemed to gain courage. She looked up at Luke, and she giggled.

'You look...*silly,*' she said.

'Gabbie!' Wendy's word was the start of a reproof but then Wendy dared herself to look at Luke, and somehow the tension dissipated and she couldn't help from grinning. 'Though, actually...'

What were they on about? 'Actually, what?' Luke asked direfully, expecting the worst. And he got it.

'You look like a derelict chimneysweep after four weeks' work with no baths in between,' she said bluntly. 'Plus... Oh, Luke, there's a scratch on your cheek that's been bleeding, and your poor leather jacket... It's ripped to pieces.'

'It's nothing,' he managed. He was so far off balance now he was practically falling over.

'It's something, Luke Grey,' she said softly, tilting her chin and meeting his look head on. 'It was absolutely something. It was the best something I've seen in a long, long while. Don't you think so, our Gabbie?'

And Gabbie's small, shy smile told them she agreed entirely.

'You do need a wash, though,' Wendy told him. 'Maybe we all do—before the electricians and glaziers and the likes arrive. Gabbie, what do you think about a swim?'

'A swim?' The child's face filled with doubt.

'A swim. Let's take a bar of soap—or maybe six bars of soap—down to the sea. We can put Grace in her carry-cot while we take Uncle Luke into the surf and we'll wash his soot off him until he looks respectable. Would you like to do that, Gabbie, love?'

'Yes,' said Gabbie definitely—and then, somehow, there was nothing left for Luke to do but follow.

Wherever they led…

CHAPTER FIVE

THE swim had been glorious, but it hadn't stopped Luke from being confused. In fact, by the end of his time in the water he was feeling so confused he wasn't sure whether he'd gone to sleep and woken in some other life.

He hadn't swum in the sea for twenty years. And now... It hadn't been a swim like he usually swam—steady laps of his local gymnasium pool designed to tone his body and make up for the days he sat at his computer, or in interminable meetings.

This had been something else. Something totally out of his ken.

They had all swum. Even Baby Grace hadn't stayed in her carry-cot for long. She'd joined right in. Wendy and Gabbie had whooped down to the sea, with Luke following behind carrying Grace. By the time he'd topped the sandhills the pair were already in the water—fully dressed!

'Because we're filthy, too.' Wendy had grinned as she'd beckoned him to join her. 'The water's warm and wonderful. Take off Grace's clothes and bring her in.'

So two minutes later he'd been sitting in the shallows, holding a naked baby on his knee—a baby who'd thought this was the most wonderful sensation she'd ever felt and it was designed for her own personal enjoyment.

And ditto for Luke. He had let Wendy and her small foster-daughter rub bars of soap though his hair and tease the grime from his face and the aches from his various bruises, and he had experienced sensations he'd never felt in his life before.

83

Despite his protests, they'd removed his shirt—'Because we can't wash it while it's on you!'—and it had only been by the resolute and determined tactic of refusing to stand up that he'd managed to keep his trousers on.

A man had some pride. Damn, he might have been waist-deep in water, and he might have been way out of depth emotionally, but if the electricians or glaziers had arrived and all he'd been wearing was boxer shorts with little red hearts on...

Good grief! The low waves broke over his legs, the girls soaped on, and he felt as if he'd been transported to another planet.

'You need antiseptic on this.' Wendy's sympathetic words jerked him back to reality—almost. The bird's claws had somehow made contact with his face. Wendy sat before him in the shallows, her skirt floating around her in the water in a soft blue swirl, and her blouse clinging much too closely.

Unaware of his reaction to her she ran a finger down the jagged scratch on his face. She'd brought a face cloth and she carefully soaped and cleaned the scratch—and the touch of her fingers on his face was enough to send him straight into orbit again. 'The salt water will be great for it,' she said softly. 'It's just what you need.'

It wasn't the salt water that was just great. This was amazing! The shallow waves ran in and out on the golden sand. The morning sun was warm on his face and on his naked chest and his bare back. Gabbie giggled and splashed beside them, and Grace wiggled her toes in the water and chortled in glee every time a wave broke over her small person.

And Wendy smiled and smiled...

'Enough!' He rose too abruptly. Grace didn't like being

hauled from her wonderful playground and she puckered her face in distress—but he had to get out of here. Now!

'There's a truck coming,' Luke said, gazing up at the house, and there was real relief in the way he said it. He might be only knee-deep in water but he was being drawn so far out of his depth that he was close to drowning. 'It'll be the electricians. I need to meet them.'

'You do that.' Wendy was watching his face from where she still sat, holding Gabbie in the water, and what she saw made her frown a little. She rose and took a step back, drawing imperceptibly away. The spell was broken. 'I'll take Grace while you go.' She reached forward and took the baby into her arms, crooning gently as she hugged her close. 'Hey, Grace, it's okay. We'll play some more.' She didn't look at Luke again. 'Off you go and organise your minions,' she told him. 'I'll come later with the children.'

'I…yes. You'll be all right?'

'I can manage,' she said softly—with dignity. 'You're the boss but we don't need you, Luke.'

And he knew, instinctively, that he was being given a deeper message than the one on the surface. But…

'I need to go.' Damn, why did he feel as if he was apologising?

'Of course you do.' She smiled, but once again he had a feeling that the shutters were being pulled closed. He'd hardly noticed they were opening, but now there was pain behind her eyes, a pain he didn't understand. She looked like a child who'd been slapped unexpectedly, and he didn't know what he'd done.

He didn't know what was causing her pain, and suddenly he wanted to. Badly.

'Wendy—'

'Go.' Her voice turned bossy—organisational—and he

knew also that this was her form of protecting herself. Why?

From emotional attachment? he wondered. Surely not. He'd kissed her once, for heaven's sake, and surely it must count as a kiss of excitement and pleasure. Not of passion. It was no big deal.

Or was it?

Well, even if it was, then it was better to move fast and leave, he told himself. Get himself into organisational mode. Now!

'I'll meet you up at the house, then,' he said neutrally. 'Later.'

'Of course.' She hugged the now wailing Grace close to her. 'Come on, Gabbie. Grace wants another swim. We'll let her have what she wants, shall we?'

'Doesn't Luke want another swim?' Gabbie asked curiously, kicking her toes out behind her in the shallows, and Wendy gave a tight little smile.

'Uncle Luke has work to do. Very important work. It's only us lucky ones who get to sit in the sea and play with our toes.'

Gabbie considered this, and slowly nodded. She turned her small face up to Luke's, and her eyes were solemn.

'I'm glad I'm not a daddy, then,' she said. 'If you can't stay and play with us, then it's sad.'

And suddenly that was exactly how Luke felt.

He was sad, and he was very, very sorry.

After that, the day passed in a blur of organisation. Luke went up to the house to meet the electrician. He showered the salt from himself and his clothes, and by the time he emerged, salt free, the glazier and the plumber had also arrived.

An hour later, when Wendy and Gabbie and Grace

trudged happily up from the beach he was almost sun dried. He was standing on the veranda discussing which of the windows were the most important to fix now, and as he saw the little procession head up from the beach he stopped mid-sentence to watch them come. The glazier turned to watch, too.

'Is that your missus and kids?' the man asked, and then, astonished, he recognised Wendy. 'Hey! That's never Wendy Maher from the kids' home?'

'Yes it is. She's staying here to care for my half-sister and her own foster-daughter. That's why I need the place to be fixed quickly.'

The man whistled. 'Well, I'll be blowed. I heard Wendy was leaving the kids' home. She's had it rough, that one, but she's *some* lady. She has a heart bigger than Africa. Why didn't you say it was for Wendy? Did I say I could only replace half a dozen windows today? If it's Wendy living here with broken windows, then I'll bring the whole team out and we'll replace the lot by dusk. That woman's a champion.'

She was.

Luke stood on the veranda and he watched them come— this tiny family he'd just created. Wendy was still sodden, her skirt and blouse clinging so he could see every gorgeous curve of her body. She was singing a silly little song and she was giggling, hugging a sleepy Grace to her very wet breast, and holding Gabbie's hand as she came, and Luke felt such a surge of emotion at the sight of them that he almost choked.

What on earth was happening to him? he demanded desperately of himself. He had to get out of here. Get a grip on himself. Now!

Getting out of here was easier than he thought. From the

tradesmen's point of view, it seemed, if the job was for Wendy then anything was possible.

So by mid-afternoon they had the electricity on, a fire was burning brightly in the stove—'The crows won't come back once we have it smoking,' Wendy told a worried Gabbie—and hot water and a phone and a clean bedroom for Wendy were organised as well.

Plus one hire car. Sort of.

'So there's nothing stopping you leaving,' Wendy told Luke, as the glazier departed with the last of his men. 'The sooner you go the sooner we can make this legal.' She eyed him doubtfully, sensing the confusion he was feeling. 'You keeping Grace, I mean.'

'Yes. I know what you mean.'

'And if you don't go now you won't get to Bay Beach Menswear before closing,' she told him. She checked him out with doubt. He'd rinsed his clothes but they'd never be respectable again. 'Just show them the colour of your money as soon as you walk in the door or they might throw you out on the spot.'

'Do I look that bad?' He rubbed his unshaven chin, and she smiled, but still with that strange, keep-your-distance look on her face.

'You look like the local wino,' she told him frankly. Then she gazed across at his hire car and her keep-your-distance attitude cracked a little as she chuckled. The newly delivered car was a vivid orange sedan—or half of it was vivid orange. The rest had been stripped, treated for rust and then painted with a strange blueish-orange undercoat. There were dents all over it. Bay Beach Motors had been right out of motors and this was the only one available. 'You match your car beautifully,' she told him.

'Gee, thanks.'

'Off you go,' she told him, and she gave him a gentle

shove toward the door. 'Your Aston Martin keys and registration papers are in the living room desk, right?'

'Right.'

'Then, I know you'll be back,' she said serenely. 'Sooner or later. Have car—will return.'

But, as Luke drove out the gate in his strange and battered jalopy, it wasn't his car he was figuring how soon he could return to.

In fact, his car was about number four on his list.

What followed was a period of peace for Wendy—but not for long.

'Tell me all. Tell me right now!'

It was three days later, and Shanni, Wendy's best friend from years back, had arrived at the farm in a state of near stupefaction. Cute, vivacious, and just returned from her extended honeymoon, Shanni was here to rescue her friend from whatever dire peril she'd put herself into, and it had taken all Wendy's counselling skills to get her to stay still and be reassured.

'There's nothing to tell.' Wendy smiled her very nicest, placating smile. 'It's just a job. You have much more exciting news. Tell me about your honeymoon. Was it good?'

'The best. But—'

'How are Nick and Harry?'

'Great, but—'

'And your new house? Is it ready for you to move into?'

'Wendy Maher, stop changing the subject.' Shanni glowered across the table. 'I leave the place for two months and what happens? I come home and my best friend is nowhere to be found—she's resigned no less!—and Erin says she's taken off with the most gorgeous man she's ever seen in her life. To live with him, in truth—*if* I have my facts right, which I can't believe I have.' She looked around her, eyes narrowing. 'Where is he?'

'I have him hidden under my bed.' Wendy chuckled. 'For use after the kids go to sleep.' Then she relented. 'No, Shanni, my boss is not here. Luke rang last night. He's in London seeing Grace's mother.'

'*In London!*' Shanni fixed her with a don't-mess-with-me look. 'Yeah, right. Your boss is in London. And he's left you here all alone. Wendy, *there's an Aston Martin in the backyard!*'

'He could hardly leave me on the farm without a car,' Wendy explained, grinning. 'It's my grocery wagon.'

Shanni gaped. 'A grocery wagon. *A brand new Aston Martin* sports car? He's never gone away and left you with it to use for groceries?'

'Of course,' she said placidly, still smiling. 'Don't all the best nannies do their grocery shopping in brand new Aston Martins?'

There was silence while Shanni took this on board. Slowly her lips compressed, and her eyes turned thoughtful. 'Nick had a sports car,' she said finally, having thought things through. 'Until he met me and Harry.'

'Well, Luke still owns a sports car.' Wendy shrugged and rose to make her friend coffee. 'Don't make a big deal of it, Shanni. He's just left it here as collateral.'

Shanni's intelligent eyes narrowed. 'Collateral. Collateral for what?'

'For him, I guess. To ensure he comes back.'

'You think otherwise he'd do a runner?'

'I have no idea,' Wendy told her. 'I have no idea in the wide world what makes Luke Grey tick.'

But still her friend eyed her thoughtfully. Then she gazed around her. Three days and an army of hired help—courtesy of Luke's credit card and enthusiastic tradesmen—had worked wonders. The house was starting to look as it once had. It was gracious and welcoming and wonderful.

And the children…

Shanni had been Gabbie's kindergarten teacher so she was one of the few people in the world Gabbie trusted. The little girl therefore decided this visit wasn't important enough to interrupt her mud pie making on the veranda. Just through the window, still in sight of her beloved Wendy, Gabbie looked busy, up to her ears in mud, and as content as a little girl could possibly be.

And in the living room through the kitchen door, Grace was snoozing peacefully on a sheepskin rug, a baby at peace with her world.

All was right for these children, Shanni thought, and from where she sat the whole place looked like something out of *Home Beautiful*—only much, much cosier.

There was so much unexplained. It was all too much for Shanni. 'Wendy, I'm going to bust if you don't come clean,' she declared. She rose, rounded the table, took her friend's shoulders and spun her around to face her. 'This place—this set-up—looks like a dream come true. There must be a catch. You tell me what's going on or I swear, I swear, I'll bust my stays.'

'As if you ever wear stays!'

'I might! We married women spread alarmingly,' her friend muttered, glowering. And then she let herself get distracted. 'Especially…especially when they're pregnant.'

'Shanni, you're not pregnant!'

'Just a little bit.' Temporarily waylaid, Shanni grinned, her happiness transparent. 'Plus we've got a new kitten called Darryl, and Nick thinks he knows where we can get a goat. So I've told you all my news. Everything. Now you tell me all, and I'm not leaving until you do. If you think

I'll leave my best friend in the power of some...*some Aston Martin driver*...'

'I'm not in his power.'

'Convince me.'

'Of course I will.'

But, at the end of a half-hour explanation—plus another half an hour of question time—Shanni rose reluctantly to leave and she wasn't convinced at all.

'How do you know he'll return?'

'Are you kidding?' Wendy motioned outside. 'Do you know how much that thing's worth? He'll be back.'

'You don't think he'd return anyway—because he loves his little sister?'

'Maybe he will in time,' Wendy said dubiously. 'But if he does love her, he doesn't know it yet.'

'So you think he'll come back, give you legal status as her nanny and then he'll go?'

'That's the plan.'

'But...he'll visit?'

'I hope he does.' Wendy didn't sound all that sure. 'It's important for Grace that he does.'

'You know...' Shanni surveyed her friend thoughtfully '...if this Luke is anything like Erin described, it'd be pretty easy to fall in love with such a man.'

'You have to be joking!'

'Stranger things have happened. Look at me and Nick.'

'I've done the love thing,' Wendy told her friend, and her voice was flat and final. 'Sure, he's cute, but there's no possibility I'm going down that road again.'

'Adam's been dead for six years.'

'And so has the baby he killed. It doesn't get one inch easier.'

'And yet you love Gabbie,' Shanni said softly, and there

was a sudden catch in her voice that she couldn't hide. Her own pregnancy had made her feel even more just how dreadful Wendy's sorrow had been, but somehow she found the courage to make herself say what had to be said.

'Wendy, you blame yourself for what happened but it hasn't stopped you loving again. You love Gabbie. I can see it every time I look at you. The way Gabbie's been treated is tearing you in two. And Grace… How much must it hurt you to lift a babe who's the same age as the baby who was killed by Adam's foolhardiness? Wendy, if you've learned to love again…'

But Wendy's face had closed. 'Loving children is different.'

'Than loving a man? Maybe. Because it was Adam who caused you such pain.' Shanni probed gently. She knew this must hurt, but it still needed to be faced. 'Not every man's like Adam, Wendy. Luke can't be blamed for Adam's mistakes.'

'Because I loved Adam too much, a child died,' Wendy said harshly. 'I should never have let him drive like that. But he was showing off—like a kid with a new toy with his damned fast car—and he was so happy! I was stupid, stupid, stupid—because I was in love—and a baby in the other car paid the price. And her parents.'

'Adam paid his price, too,' Shanni reminded her. 'He's dead. It's over, Wendy.'

'Yes, it's over.' Wendy turned and sat down at the table, and her shoulders slumped. 'I know. It's finished. But I loved Adam too much, and I lost control. I will never, *ever* feel like that again. I'll love my children, I'll protect them, and that's all.'

'Wendy…'

'For heaven's sake, Luke's way out of my league anyway,' Wendy told her, trying to smile. 'He's rich, he spends his life abroad, and he's gorgeous. What would a man like that want with the likes of me?'

Which was just what Luke Grey was asking of himself at that very minute.

Ten thousand miles away, Luke was face to face with Grace's mother, and suddenly, inexplicably, he wanted Wendy with him. Right now!

Lindy was gorgeous. How had his father—a man who'd been in his late sixties—ever attracted a woman like this? Luke checked out the woman who he'd finally tracked down in one of London's best hotels, and he could find no answer. Sure, his father had charm, but one glance told him this was a lady accustomed to the best that money could buy, and then some.

He'd discovered by now that she was a model, and it showed. Lindy was almost six feet tall; she was willow-slim, with fabulous chestnut curls draped ever so carefully down to her breasts. Each curl looked individually arranged. Her eyes were sky-blue, huge and wondrous. Her rosebud lips were pouting prettily at her unexpected visitor, and her gorgeous, gold kimono looked as if it was straight from a designer's collection.

She must have cost his father a mint, Luke thought cynically. No wonder the old man had died in so much debt. But why did one look at her make him feel like running a mile?

'You didn't need to come all this way to find me,' Lindy told him, and her voice was carefully modulated to a sexy whisper. Luke's mistrust deepened. He knew that this was the way she'd speak to any attractive man in her orbit.

'I had quite a time finding you,' Luke admitted, hauling himself into business mode. It was the only way to cope here. 'Someone in your modelling agency gave me a break and told me where you were.'

Her eyes flared with anger. 'They shouldn't have. I told them...'

'You really didn't want me to find you?' Luke asked curiously. 'You honestly don't want anything more to do with your daughter?'

'I didn't want her to start with,' she said petulantly. 'Your father did, and he caught me at a low moment. My modelling career was going through a dive, and all my friends were having babies, so I thought, well, why not? Babies look so cute, and your father told me there'd always be enough money for the best nannies.'

Not the best, Luke thought involuntarily. He had the best nanny in the world—right back in Bay Beach. Where he wanted to be right now...

'But then—your father died and there was nothing.' The girl's voice had lost its sexy whisper as her distress showed through. Distress and anger. This wasn't grief for his father, Luke decided. This was distress because she'd been cheated out of cash.

'He'd promised there'd be money for ever, and there was nothing,' she continued. 'Nothing! They kicked me out of my apartment—which I thought we owned! My nanny left because I couldn't pay her. So there I was, alone, and I'd never even changed the kid's nappy. Suddenly I had to do everything. I hated it. Then, just as I hit rock bottom I got a call from the agency saying they had this job for me. Touring with the whole Europe collection. I'll be in Europe for three months now—or even longer if my plans go right. You must see, I can't have the kid.'

'You can't have Grace while you're touring,' Luke agreed quietly—so quietly that those who knew him well would recognise the danger signs. There was deep distaste in his voice. 'Will you want her back afterwards?'

Lindy's huge eyes widened in surprise, as if such a question was self-evident. 'Why on earth would I?'

'She's your daughter.'

'No.' The woman shook her gorgeous mane of hair in quick decision. 'That's not how I feel about her. I was used. I was lied to. I was conned into having her and I want no responsibility for her future.'

'She's still very cute,' Luke said, watchful.

'Yeah? You try getting up at two in the morning night after night and see how cute she is. And the cost of nannies...' Lindy's face suddenly stilled, intelligence sharpening and focusing right on Luke. 'But you must be rich. The guy I hired to find you said you were some sort of stockbroker, and if you can afford to come all the way to London to find me... If you pay for a nanny and something toward our keep then I might consider it.'

Her eyes narrowed, dollar signs lighting up in their depths. 'I mean, it was your father who cheated me. You owe it to me.'

'I owe you *nothing*.' He'd had enough. Luke's face was tight and hard. The thought of his half-sister with *this* woman was making his blood boil. 'I'm not legally obliged to care for any other children my father might have had besides me.'

'I know that,' she snapped. 'My lawyer said I couldn't touch you. But she is your half-sister.'

'And if I don't look after her?'

'Then I'll get her adopted,' Lindy said brutally. 'I tell you, I can't have her. What man's going to look at me when I have a kid in tow?'

And that was the crux of the matter, Luke thought bleakly. Grace had no chance at all.

'If I agree to take her...' he said slowly—cautiously.

'Will you?' Her eyes widened again, clearly surprised, and Luke took a mental step back. It'd be dangerous for this woman to think he cared.

'I have...I care for another child,' he told her, and her face relaxed again, turning into a sneer.

'Do you, now? How about that? I might have known. Like father, like son.'

'As you say,' he said neutrally. It wouldn't hurt negotiations if Lindy thought he was heartless. 'But I've thought it through and made a decision. If you really want to be rid of Grace, then I'll take care of your daughter—out of memory for my father.'

She stared at him then, surprised. 'You didn't inherit that sort of conscience from your old man,' she said, and a note of pleading suddenly entered her lovely voice. 'That'd be great. If you would...'

'If that's what you want, then I need to be appointed her legal guardian,' Luke told her. 'If you really do want me to keep her.'

'I don't want to sign anything.' She backed a step.

'But I can't take care of her without the legal right to do so,' Luke said carefully—smoothly. 'I've had legal advice. I need your official custody agreement.'

'No.'

He sighed, but he'd come prepared. 'I'm sorry, Lindy, but we can't leave it like this. The way things are, Grace is in limbo, with me having no legal rights to care for her and you not wanting her.'

'So what?'

His face hardened, but forewarned by Wendy—and his lawyers—he'd come prepared to play it tough. 'Then maybe we need to go public,' he said softly, watching her

changing expressions. 'Let the press know that you abandoned your daughter.'

Her face paled. 'You wouldn't.'

'All I want is for you to give me legal jurisdiction to
care for her,' he said again, remembering Wendy. He
needed to protect Wendy in all this. 'Then I'll take on your
responsibility and you don't need to worry.'

'But...' the woman bit her lip '...I might—'

'Change your mind?' Luke's angry expression softened,
just a little. 'Lindy, the woman who's looking after your
daughter now is a social worker,' he told her. 'She's the
best—and she's told me that as she gets older Grace will
need contact with you as much or more than you do with
her. Even if it's only spasmodic. We can write access into
any custody arrangement. That way, you'll always know
where she is, and if you wish to see her then you may.'

'But not take her back?'

'That's right.' With Wendy's advice still ringing in his
ears, he made his final ultimatum. 'It's not fair on Grace
to do anything else. If you wish me to take on responsibility—and Grace's expenses—for the rest of her life, I'm
willing to do it, but only when it's made legal.'

Lindy stared at him for one long, hard minute.

'You know, you really are very cute,' she said slowly—
surprisingly—checking him out from the toes up. 'You
don't suppose...?'

'I don't suppose anything,' Luke said harshly. Heck, the
woman scared him. More and more he was thinking long-
ingly of Wendy. Wendy of the flowery skirts and the wispy
curls and the mystical, caring quality that was light years
away from this woman's glamour. 'If you agree, then I'll
meet with you and my lawyers in the morning. Yes?'

She chewed her pretty lip for all of three seconds. This

was obviously no bigger decision than deciding what colour nail polish to put on.

'Yes,' she said finally. 'And then I can get on with my life.'

'The Aston Martin's still here, I see.'

Wendy was digging up weeds from an overgrown rose garden. Shanni had come on her by surprise, and now she sank down to sit in the sun beside her friend. 'So when does Wonder Boy return?'

'Maybe Tuesday.'

'Tuesday.' Shanni nodded. 'Can I meet him?'

Wendy sighed and stopped digging. 'He's my boss, Shanni. Not my friend. So no, you can't meet him. He may only be here for an hour or so. He's bringing Grace's custody papers and a legal employment contract for me. After that, he's free to go where he will.'

'He's adopting Grace?'

'So it seems.' Wendy sat back on her heels and regarded her cleared earth with pride. After so much hard work, the house and garden were starting to look great. 'It's surprised me, too,' she admitted, 'but there it is. He's willing not just to take on her care, but to take on her care for ever. He rang from London yesterday. The adoption won't be formally through for three months. Lindy can change her mind any time in that three months but he's pretty sure she won't. He's taken the first steps and he's now Grace's legal carer.'

'So he has a baby for ever?'

'Yes.'

'And you...' Shanni eyed her friend sideways. Sitting here in the sun, she'd never seen her friend looking so content. So at peace with her world. For once, things were turning out right for Wendy, and it pleased Shanni to the socks. 'You might just have a job and a home for ever.'

'I doubt our Mr Grey wants to be saddled with a baby by his side as he jets round the world doing very important things,' Wendy said contentedly. 'After all, he's an international man of business.'

'And you're content to stay and keep the home fires burning while he jets?'

'Shanni, this arrangement gives Gabbie a home,' Wendy murmured. As they spoke, Gabbie was crawling out from under a bush that she'd decreed was her cubby house. Away from the tensions of the orphanage—from the pressures involved in housing half a dozen children from disturbed backgrounds—the little girl was blooming by the minute. She was growing braver and braver. 'My Gabbie has a gorgeous little sister, and she has me,' Wendy said softly, watching her. 'That's worth a million. Or more!'

And you have a home, too, Shanni thought with pleasure, though she didn't say it. That had to be worth even more.

But overwhelmingly Shanni was aching to meet this unknown Luke—this wonder man who'd provided this happy-ever-after setting for her friend. Because Shanni's sharp mind was asking all sorts of silent questions. After all, this house had everything it needed for a family—except for one thing.

Hmm.

CHAPTER SIX

LUKE arrived home at midnight on Monday night. Home…

He pulled into the farm driveway and stared up at the darkened house, feeling a gut-wrenching gladness at reaching his destination that he hadn't felt since he was a child. This really was his home.

Hell, he'd never realised how much he'd missed it.

The place looked somehow different than when he'd left, even in semi-darkness. The moon was almost full, and he could see the ancient rose bushes around the front entrance had been pruned back, and the garden beds had been dug over. The last of the boarding over the windows had been removed. There was gleaming glass in every frame, and there were curtains behind the glass. The place looked clean and welcoming, and a couple of old chairs had been dragged outside onto the veranda so one could sit outside and watch the distant surf.

It looked great!

Quietly he climbed from the car, stretching weary limbs. A twenty-four hour flight followed by a spot of urgent shopping and a huge drive on top was a bit much for anyone. He should have stayed overnight in the city, he acknowledged, but he'd felt such a compulsion to be here… And besides, there was Bruce.

They'd be asleep, he thought, as Bruce was now sleeping, but he knew where they'd be. He wouldn't disturb them.

Taking off his shoes he made his way softly up to the veranda. Through the living room to the kitchen beyond.

'Visitors should ring doorbells,' Wendy said from behind him and he jumped about a foot. It was all he could do not to yelp.

Somehow he lost his voice as he wheeled to face her. That was a shock again. Wendy was wearing her gorgeous, faded nightgown, and her curls were tumbling free around her bare shoulders. Baby Grace was lying in her arms as she stood in the doorway between kitchen and living room. By the moonlight flooding through the French windows, Wendy's face was tender and somehow vulnerable—and she was such a contrast from the woman he'd left in London that for the life of him Luke couldn't think of another thing to say.

But she took pity on him and broke the silence. 'I guess you're not really a visitor.' She smiled, and motioned to the sleeping baby she was cradling. 'Don't turn on the light. I've just got her settled.'

'Is she...?' Luke moved forward in the moonlight, peering down at his half-sister. She was deeply asleep, her tiny mouth curved into a smile of such bliss that Luke's heart twisted. 'Is she...okay?'

'What do you think?' Wendy chuckled softly into the stillness. 'She shouldn't be having a bottle in the middle of the night, but do you think I can persuade her of that? This young lady has a mind of her own—like her brother, I'd say. She's just got her own way—*again*—and very pleased she is, too.'

'I...see.' He didn't. For some reason his brain was all fuzzy. But luckily Wendy appeared not to notice.

'And now it's bedtime, miss,' she was telling Grace. 'For the whole night!' Wendy fixed the sleeping baby with a look of stern warning, but the tenderness behind her eyes gave her warning the lie. The stirring in Luke's gut grew deeper. This feeling he was experiencing. It wasn't just his baby sister doing the damage here, he decided. Help!

But Wendy's attention was still not on him. She was concentrating solely on getting Grace back to bed without her waking. 'Wait,' she told him softly. 'I'll just be a minute.'

Without another word she turned and carried the sleeping Grace out to her bedroom. He waited silently. There was nothing else to do, and to stay completely still, letting the atmosphere of the beloved old house seep into his bones, suited him very well until she padded barefoot back—to where he was waiting with the same look of stunned confusion on his face that she'd left him with.

Then she flicked on a table lamp, and his mixed emotions grew even more muddled. Even more lopsided.

He stared around at the transformed kitchen in amazement. 'What on earth have you done to this place?'

She smiled at that. 'I scrubbed it,' she said proudly. '*And* I painted the walls. I don't mean to boast, but it looks great, doesn't it?'

It certainly did. When Luke had left, the kitchen had been grimy and dreary from years of neglect, and in the few days he'd been away Wendy had totally transformed it. The stove was gleaming, and the table and old wooden benches had been scrubbed to within an inch of their lives. The walls had been painted a pretty powder blue and there were fresh gingham curtains hanging in the window. It looked…wonderful.

'You did all this?' He could hardly believe it.

'With the help of your credit card.' Wendy's smile was teasing. 'Elbow-grease and money. What a combination!' Then her smile faded. 'Did you get what we needed from Lindy?'

He nodded, lifting the precious documents from his

breast pocket. But he wasn't thinking about papers. He was having trouble thinking past Wendy. She was so incredibly lovely. So incredibly *desirable*.

She was so…Wendy!

Hell! He was acting like a moron here. With a wrench he hauled his thoughts back to the subject she was interested in. Documents. Grace. Not him.

'Lindy's signed the pre-adoption papers,' he told her. 'She did it in London, in the presence of two lawyers and a witness from the embassy. If she doesn't change her mind in the cooling off period—and I'd be amazed if she does—then Grace will be ours.' He faltered then at the look on her face, and he was suddenly uncertain of his ground. 'I mean—'

'You mean she'll be *yours*,' Wendy said gently. 'Remember, I'm just the nanny.'

'I…yes. I guess.' He was all at sea here. He was trying to concentrate on Grace's adoption, but all he could see was Wendy. She was so gorgeous—so sexy!—it was all he could do not to lunge around the table and take her into his arms for a passionate kiss.

'Your bed's made up in your grandparents' room,' she said placidly, as if unaware of the crazy mix of emotions charging around the room all by themselves. 'At least, we assumed it was your grandparents' room. The big front one with the double bed.'

'Yes.'

'It should be okay,' she told him. 'There's clean linen and bedding. The only thing is…'

'There's a problem?'

She grinned. 'Well, there's sort of two bumps that you'll have to straddle. I'd assume at a guess that you're a lot bigger than your grandpa.'

That shook him. He didn't have a clue what she was talking about. 'Two bumps?'

'I'd bet your grandma and grandpa had the same bed for their entire married lives,' she told him cheerfully. 'Gabbie and I made the bed up yesterday and you can see exactly where they slept. There's deep contours linked together at the hip where they've lain side by side for years.' The tenderness returned to her face. 'I guess it won't be too comfortable for one big person sleeping in the bed, but I don't know. The bumps look…sort of…nice.'

It was nice at that, Luke thought, and blinked. His grandparents… Two lovers lying side by side, making their indentations in their mattress night after night as they slept—husband and wife for forty years. Why did the thought have the capacity to kick him sideways?

But he hauled his thoughts back together again. Somehow.

'It'll be fine.' His voice was gruffer than he meant it to be and, for a minute she stared, sensing his confusion.

Then she too pulled herself together. Maybe she was starting to feel the emotion zooming around the room like electricity searching for a grounding. Maybe.

Or maybe she just thought he was a moron.

'Can I make you a cup of tea before I go back to bed? Or can you manage on your own?' She wanted to leave, he could see. Grace had woken her from sleep and now she wanted to slip back into her own bed and sleep again—alone. As was right and proper. He was her boss. She was his hired nanny.

But still he wanted to prolong the moment. Desperately. 'How's…how's Gabbie?' he asked.

As a delaying tactic, it was a good ploy. Her face softened. 'Gabbie is great. Just great,' she told him. 'She loves this place, just like me.' She smiled up at him with gratitude and the instinct to kiss her surfaced again and then some.

'I brought her a present.' His voice was gruff again. Too gruff. Stupid!

'A present?'

'I…' He was stammering like a schoolboy, and that was how she made him feel. As if he was about thirteen years old—a schoolboy suffering his first serious crush. 'It's in the car. I need to bring it in straight away.'

'Won't it wait until morning?' She was confused, and still she was intent on getting back to her bed. Away from him. 'Gabbie's asleep. A gift can wait.'

'I might be only driving a hire car,' he told her firmly—a man had some standards! 'But I hate to imagine what even that would look like if I left this until tomorrow morning. No, Miss Maher…' he somehow managed to smile at her confusion '…I won't take you up on your offer of a cup of tea, but I'd appreciate very much if you could heat a little hot milk. I'll fetch Bruce now.'

'Bruce?'

'I know I keep doing it,' he said apologetically. 'I just can't seem to help myself. I'm sorry, Wendy, but I've brought you another baby!'

'What?' Her jaw dropped about a foot and he grinned at her reaction.

'Just wait and see.'

He hadn't known what to expect.

On the plane on the way to England he'd thought of this and it had seemed the most wonderful idea. He'd rung his Australian secretary while he'd been in London; she'd done all the legwork while he'd been talking Lindy into signing adoption papers, and when he'd landed back in Australia it had been organised so all he'd had to do was go and pick Bruce up and pay unseemly amounts of money.

At his first sight of Bruce it had seemed an even better idea. Bruce was…well, Bruce was just Bruce from the first moment he'd seen him. For a man unaccustomed to falling in love at first sight—or even love at all—Luke had come pretty close when he'd met Bruce.

But now, carrying the sleeping puppy into the kitchen, he had his first major doubt. What if Wendy didn't like dogs? What if she hated animals? What if…?

And then his worst fears were confirmed.

He entered the kitchen and put the tiny, still sleepy and befuddled basset-hound puppy down onto the kitchen floor. Bruce stared up at his new surroundings in amazement, and he was all eyes and ears and tummy.

What next? Wendy stared down at the puppy in stunned silence. The puppy stared back at Wendy for one long moment, and then, sensing a mother figure and smelling the warming milk, he waddled solemnly forward—so his dangling ears were brushing the hem of Wendy's nightgown and his huge eyes were gazing straight up at her. His small liver-and-white-spotted person quivered with anxiety. He looked and looked, and his tiny, whip-like tail slowly started to rotate in canine hopefulness.

She had to like him. To Luke, watching in silence, Bruce Basset looked almost irresistible.

But Wendy stooped down to floor level without saying a word. She touched Bruce lightly on his velvety ears—and she burst into tears.

Hell! This was appalling. What to do now? Of all things—to have made Wendy cry…

'You don't have to keep him. I didn't mean… If you think I've already dumped enough on you I can take him back.' Luke started forward, but then he paused as the puppy was scooped up into Wendy's arms and she glared up at Luke as if she was a mother hen protecting her entire brood.

'Take him back?' Her voice was laced with emotion and tears were slipping down her face unchecked and unheeded. 'Take him back? Don't you dare!'

'But...' Hell, she was *crying!* 'Don't you like him? Wendy, what's wrong?' Unconsciously he stooped too, so his eyes were on a level with hers. The puppy was squirming in her arms, and his small pink tongue came out to lick away a tear.

Hey, the puppy knew what to do. Luke grabbed his handkerchief and moved in to help. Now there were two males attending to Wendy's tears and it was all too much. Wendy was falling backwards, sitting on the floor and sobbing helplessly into Bruce's velvety coat.

But she was also...smiling? Laughing through tears? Luke managed to get a piece of his handkerchief to her cheeks. It was licked aside by the puppy and, hell, he was jealous of a puppy!

'You *don't* want me to take him back?' he tried cautiously and now he was sure she'd been chuckling. She was smiling at him through her tears and her eyes were shining like raindrops in a sunshower. She hugged the crazy, wriggling bundle of puppy, and she smiled and smiled—and Luke's heart lurched as if it had never lurched in its life before.

'Luke, if you knew how much I'd wanted to give Gabbie a puppy...' It was all she could do to get her voice to a whisper. She hugged Bruce again, venting her overstrung emotions on his small squiggly person. 'We have Home dogs—specially trained dogs skilled in being hugged by children in need—and Gabbie's loved them. But they've never been hers, and every time she's moved it's been to a different dog. But this little one… She needs something to love so much…'

'And you do, too,' he said thoughtfully, watching her face. Somewhere inside something was starting to feel really, really good. He'd done something right! He'd made this woman happy. Luke Grey, independent mover and shaker, had made this lady happy.

And it felt—fantastic!

'And me too,' she admitted shyly. She lifted the little dog high so woman and dog were nose to nose. 'I admit it. I haven't owned a dog since I was a child, and I've wanted one so much. Now I have Gabbie and I have Grace, and I have Bruce.' She turned to look at him with exactly the same look she'd bestowed on Bruce. Unswerving love. 'Oh, Luke, thank you. I don't know how to say it…'

'You don't need to.'

'But Luke…'

'No.' He reached forward and caught a last errant tear, whisking it away with his forefinger.

And then suddenly he was so close. She was so lovely. God help him, a man would have to be inhuman to resist a sight like this.

He wasn't inhuman. This lady before him was Wendy. Wendy! She'd been weeping and she was so, so near…

He moved just inches closer. She gazed at him with eyes that were loving and misty with tears, and his fingers caught her under the chin.

Some things were just inevitable. He kissed her.

And wow!

Heaven knew what went into that kiss. It was a kiss that had the power to change the world—or change the world of the two persons whose lips touched—and change the world it did.

She was so gorgeous. So…

Her lips were just as he'd known they would be. Just as he'd remembered from that fleeting kiss with the children between them. They were full and soft and warm and yielding—and tasting slightly of salt where the tears had slid unchecked.

The puppy was still there, somewhere between them, but his small warm presence did not intrude. He'd been woken from sleep, but a pup could tell these two soft bodies meant a small creature nothing but good. It was clear that Bruce believed he was on to a very good thing here...

As did Luke. Wendy felt so wonderful. It was all part of the magic of the night, he thought. It was part of the discovery of coming home. Home...

Here was his home.

Wendy was his home.

The discovery was no lightning bolt. It was more a sweet, insidious knowledge, creeping softly into his consciousness. He'd never known what he was missing until this moment, but here, in this moonlit kitchen, with the soft wuffling of a puppy between them, he found a missing link in his life that he hadn't known was broken.

And Wendy?

For the life of her she couldn't pull away. The knowledge that was already with Luke was playing its magic part on her as well. It was like a spell, numbing her brain, making her unaware of anything but how good this man felt, how strong were the hands that gripped her shoulders—how warm was the mouth on hers...

How achingly empty her life was without...

Without what? A man?

Dear God. Where had that thought come from? It slammed into her brain like a zillion volts and it scared her rigid. Of all the stupid, stupid things to think...

Luke was still kissing her—she was still letting herself

be kissed—but suddenly things weren't the same. The numbness had worn off. She'd been down this road before, letting emotion sway her... Letting hormones do their thing until she'd risked so much she had no right to risk!

No!

'No!'

Heaven knew how she uttered the word. Heaven knew how there was enough space between them to say it but somehow, somehow she dragged herself back, and her eyes were fear-filled and dreadful.

He let her go. 'Love, what is it?'

What had he called her? *Love?* He had to be joking.

'What on earth do you think you're doing?' She clutched the puppy to her. Bruce looked up in faint reproach; it had been really cosy cradled between chest and breast, and he wouldn't have minded staying there!

Luke's voice, when he found it, was a bit shaken. 'I thought I was kissing you.' Somehow he managed a faint chuckle. 'And I thought you were kissing me right back.'

'It must have been the puppy.' She gasped and scrambled to her feet. 'I wouldn't...'

'You wouldn't have kissed me? Liar!'

'Luke!' There was real distress in her voice and he heard it. A frown creased his eyes.

'Wendy, what's wrong?'

'This...this is ridiculous.'

'Us kissing?'

'Yes.' She took a jagged breath, searching for control. 'Ridiculous,' she repeated. 'You're my boss. We have a business relationship.'

'A business relationship?'

'Yes. Nothing more.' She closed her eyes and hugged Bruce closer. 'Nothing else. Otherwise it'd be...a disaster.'

He nodded, watching her face. If he took one step closer

to her now she'd run, he knew, and he also knew quite desperately that the last thing he wanted was for this woman to run. And it wasn't for the sake of two small children and one puppy...

Keep it light, he told himself. He'd scared her. What woman had ever reacted like this to him kissing her? he asked himself, but Wendy was doing just that, and it was Wendy he wanted most desperately to stay. So he had to learn some new rules. Fast.

'I always kiss women who weep,' he said, making his voice light. 'It serves you right for turning on the water-works.'

'I didn't cry.'

'Ha!'

'I just...I just got a bit emotional when I saw the puppy.'

She was playing for lightness, too. Good. They could take it from here.

'Great. Soggy puppy. Soggy woman. I have a houseful.'

'He's...' She'd withdrawn, but she had herself almost under control and she was searching for a safer topic. 'He's really for Gabbie?'

'He's really for Gabbie.' He gave her an encouraging grin. 'But not tonight. If we give him some milk now he can sleep in my room.'

She looked up at him, startled, and he gave a mocking smile. 'Now, why does that surprise you?'

Her brow creased. 'I guess I had you down as the sort of guy who'd say put him on the veranda to sleep.'

'Yeah, right.' He had his voice almost completely back under control now. Pity about his emotions. 'I tried that. Or sort of.'

'What do you mean?'

'I put him in a cardboard box when I picked him up from the dealer. I put him on the back seat for the drive here and it lasted exactly five minutes. First of all he howled so much I sounded like a police car belting down the freeway, and then he proceeded to eat the cardboard box. Once the box was eaten, he threw up, then kept right on howling.'

'Oh, Luke!' The tension of moments ago was passing. Almost. He had her chuckling. 'So what did you do?'

'What any sane man had to do,' Luke said, sighing. 'He spent the remainder of the trip on my knee, which is a totally illegal, dangerous but admittedly peaceable way to carry a dog. About half an hour from here he fell into such a deep sleep that he fell sideways and upside down onto the passenger seat, but even then he kept an eye on me. So if I stick him on the veranda, what's the chance of us getting any sleep at all tonight?'

'Somewhere about zero, I'd say,' Wendy agreed, grinning, and Luke nodded.

'Well, there you go, then. You have your baby for the night and I have mine. Opposite ends of the house and I hope my baby doesn't need feeding any more than yours. And I hope to high heaven mine doesn't snore.'

He did.

Bruce snored happily well into morning, wuffling contentedly in a basket right underneath where Luke lay. He snuffled and snorted and it was enough to drive a man mad—but then, to be fair, maybe it wasn't Bruce who was driving him nuts. Maybe he was feeling he was going nuts anyway.

Above, on his grandparents' lumpy bed, Luke lay awake and stared into the darkness, searching for answers that weren't there. He didn't know why he was feeling like he was. He didn't even know for sure how he was feeling! All he knew was that every time he saw Wendy she had the power to shift his world on its axis.

He wanted her so much it was a physical ache.

Why?

She wasn't his sort of woman, he told himself over and over. How would she fit into his life?

She wouldn't. He couldn't see her entertaining his sophisticated friends back in the city, but then... Suddenly the thought of entertaining his sophisticated friends didn't seem so desirable any more. Not when the alternative was being here.

Being with Wendy.

It was a passing phase, he told himself desperately, rolling over and thumping his pillow as if it was personally responsible. It was just that he'd never met anyone like Wendy before, and she was a novelty. It'd wear off. If he spent a bit more time here...

Hmm. A bit more time here... He turned the idea over in his mind and he liked it.

Well, why not? What was so urgent back in the city, after all? He had his laptop computer here—he never travelled without it. He had his mobile phone. He could set up one of the spare bedrooms as an office, hook up an internet connection and really get to know this place again. Get to know Grace and Gabbie. Play with Bruce.

Get Wendy out of his system.

Yeah, right.

Well, a man could only try. Underneath his bed, Bruce snuffled again in sleep, nosing round anxiously for another of his litter. He really was being incredibly brave for a puppy having his first night away from his mum, and Luke's heart went out to him. His hand dropped down from the bed to fondle the little dog's ears, and next minute

Bruce ended up right in there beside him, snuggled into his grandmother's bump.

'I'm no soft option here,' Luke warned him. 'I don't do attachment.'

Bruce wuffled his agreement and a warm pink tongue came out and licked his face from jaw to nose. Then the little dog snuggled closer.

I don't do attachment…

'What the hell am I letting myself in for?' Luke demanded of him. 'Do you have a clue?'

But there was only silence, and then, finally, Bruce's soft puppy snoring as the little dog slept.

Luke was left to figure things out alone.

Damn, he was tired. He should sleep. He *must* sleep!

How could a man sleep when in the other end of the house there was Wendy?

Not that Wendy was getting any sleep, either. While Luke tossed and turned and had useless conversations with one small canine, Wendy was doing pretty much the same with the sleeping Grace.

'He's dangerous, your brother,' she told the snoozing infant. 'Of all the stupid things to do, to let him kiss me…'

Unconsciously her fingers came up to her lips, tracing the pressure Luke had placed on her mouth. It had felt just wonderful—*right!* As if it was meant to happen.

'Which is stupid!' she told herself fiercely. 'I don't get attached. I'm *not* interested in men in general, nor one man in particular. I am especially not in the market for some short-term fling that will mess up my future, and I sure as hell don't want anything more than a short-term fling.'

She sighed and thought it through, and when she spoke again some of the bitterness was gone, leaving only bleakness.

'Not that he's offering anything more,' she told the dark. 'Luke's a man who takes what he wants when he wants it. Anyone can see that. He's rich and he travels and he's here for a night or so and then gone. Gone! So, Wendy Maher, you can take what your crazy emotions are telling you, and you can go wash those feelings down the sink with some ice water. Get a grip on yourself, woman. Right now!'

Which was all very well, she told herself an hour later, and an hour after that. It was all very well, but it was totally impractical advice when all she could think of was how that kiss had felt.

Impossible!

Finally she rose and crossed to look out the window to the sea beyond. Luke's precious car was parked just below the veranda and the sight of that extravagance helped her resolve.

'He's like Adam,' she whispered. 'They all are. Men! And if you let him get close—if you let emotions muck up your employee-employer relationship—then you'll need to leave this wonderful place that's so right for Gabbie, and you won't be able to take care of Grace any longer.'

'That's right.'

'So be sensible.'

'Yes, ma'am,' she told her wayward heart. She sighed again and went back to bed.

But not to sleep.

CHAPTER SEVEN

THE howling could be heard in the next continent. It went on and on, an awful, dismal, baying loneliness, filling the house, ringing out toward the sea, dreadful and searing in its intensity.

Luke, who was sleeping right beside it, woke as if he'd been shot.

Wendy, who was dozing fitfully, stirred and winced and reached automatically into the cradle beside her bed, in a swift gesture of comfort for the baby. But it wasn't her baby who was doing the howling.

And in the next-door boxroom, Gabbie sat bolt upright at the sound, gave a whimper of fright and made a frantic dive straight underneath Wendy's bedcovers. From there she poked up a quivering nose and ventured to ask, 'What is it? What is it?' The child was trembling like a leaf. 'Wendy...'

'It's nothing to be afraid of.' Boy, Bruce could wake the dead, here. Wendy suppressed a sigh. 'Uncle Luke came home—came back last night—and he has a surprise for you. I'd imagine that's what the noise is.'

Gabbie's nose emerged another inch or two from under the quilt. Tucked up in bed with Wendy, she was brave enough—sort of. 'A surprise?'

'That's what I said.'

'For me?'

'Go take a look. You know where Luke will be sleeping. Or trying to sleep.'

Nobody could be sleeping now. Even Grace was stirring.

117

The howl sounded on and on into the dawn, and Gabbie's fingers clutched Wendy's.

'That's the surprise?' Her eyes were like saucers. 'It sounds awful.'

'It's not awful. Go see.'

Gabbie gulped. 'Not without you.'

Now how had she known she'd say that? With a sigh, Wendy hauled back the bedcovers and poked her feet into her slippers. She pulled on a robe—at least she could be respectable here—and then took Gabbie's hand. A gurgle from the crib reminded them both that they weren't a pair. They were a team.

'Grace wants to see, too,' Gabbie announced and Wendy nodded.

'Of course. Why not.' She lifted the baby, and Grace's bright button eyes twinkled up at her. 'Your big brother is home,' she told her. 'And he's brought our Gabbie a present. A present that's intent on breaking the sound barrier. Okay, team. Let's go meet this present before it splits our eardrums.'

The puppy was not happy.

Last night things had been different and interesting and exhausting for a pup. First there had been the initial meeting with Luke—an hour while he'd played and rolled and generally talked his way into a new owner's heart. Then he'd been put into a cardboard box which had taken all of one small dog's ingenuity and energy to escape from. There'd been some very interesting tummy collywobbles—courtesy of cardboard consumption—and by the time he'd arrived at Bay Beach, met Wendy, been given warm milk and been put to bed, the small Bruce had been so exhausted that he'd slept all night.

But now he'd woken in a strange bed, with a strange

person and there wasn't another basset-hound in sight. No mum. No brothers and sisters. It was enough to freak a small pup right out, and freak Bruce did, at the top of his lungs. His howl went on for ever, no matter how much Luke picked him up and told him he was okay and offered him puppy food and anything else a small dog could desire.

He wanted none of it. He howled and he howled and he howled.

And that was how Wendy and Gabbie and Grace found him. Still howling. They opened Luke's bedroom door with caution, and Luke was sitting up looking resplendent in pale blue pyjamas with bright red sailing boats all over—he'd made a special effort to make up for the red-hearted boxer shorts—and Bruce was sitting on his knee, his small basset nose was raised to the moon, and he was howling with all the gusto of generation after generation of basset-hound ancestors—and maybe a bit of wolf ancestry thrown in for good measure.

Wendy stopped dead at the sight before her. There was Luke in his sailing-boat pyjamas, helplessly holding a howling basset puppy. They looked truly, truly ridiculous! Oh, dear...

She'd never seen a man look so helpless. One man in charge of his world—but not in charge of one small puppy. 'Oh...'

By her side, Gabbie breathed deeply, awestruck at the sight. She took in the scene, and her mouth dropped wide open. 'It's a puppy,' she whispered. 'A puppy!'

'It's a very noisy puppy,' Wendy said, but she wasn't sure she could be heard over the racket. She knelt so she could hear what Gabbie was saying.

'Why is it crying?' Gabbie whispered, still clutching Wendy's hand as if Bruce might leap on her, fangs bared. Ha!

'I guess he's missing his mummy.'

'Then where's his mummy?' Gabbie's big eyes flew to Luke, and suddenly there was accusation behind them.

'Hey, I didn't steal his mother,' Luke said, wounded. He could see straight away what she was thinking. 'He was being sold anyway.'

'He was being sold?'

'Puppies need owners,' Wendy told her gently, giving her a small and gentle push forward. 'Your Uncle Luke decided that this puppy's owner would be you. I guess that means, from now on, you're the puppy's mummy. If that's what you want.'

'Oh…' The little girl's breath sighed out in a long, jagged rush of awe. 'Oh…'

'If you want him,' Wendy said. She gave a rueful look at Bruce, who's nose was still in the air, whose ears were back and who was still howling at the moon as if there was no tomorrow. Oh, dear. Maybe…maybe a basset-hound wasn't such a great choice.

But…

'I can be his mummy?' Gabbie whispered.

'He needs a mummy.' It was Luke now, speaking above the noise. He cast an uncertain glance at Wendy and then focused on Gabbie. This was important. 'I tried to act like his mum last night but I'm not very good at it. See…he doesn't think I make the grade.'

'How can I be his mummy?' Gabbie seemed totally befuddled.

'You might try cuddling him and giving him some breakfast,' Wendy suggested.

'Mmm.'

For a long, long moment the little girl considered this, while, unconcerned with these stupid humans, the puppy howled on. Then, appearing at last to come to a decision,

Gabbie solemnly released Wendy's hand. She walked those last few steps forward, and put her hand on the puppy's head.

'Don't cry, puppy,' she said.

The puppy cast her a doubtful look—and went right on howling.

But instinctively Gabbie knew what to do. She took a deep breath, took her courage in both hands and lifted the puppy up until her eyes met his.

'Hey, puppy, this is a good place to be,' she told him, and her voice was even a little stern. 'This is a place for people without mummies. Grace and me don't have mummies and Wendy's our mummy and it's really good here. And if you like, I'll be your mummy and we'll have fun together. And you can play in my cubby.'

There was suddenly silence. Miraculously there was silence. The whole world held its breath while Bruce seemed to consider his options.

Wendy and Luke's eyes met, and they held their collective breath.

Girl and dog were nose to nose. The puppy eyeballed his new mistress for a long, long moment—and then, very slowly, the tiny tail stirred and waved.

And one pink tongue came out for this final investigation. Tongue met nose. Bruce was meeting his new mistress. His...mummy? And Luke looked up at Wendy and grinned and grinned, as if he'd personally achieved a miracle.

Which, come to think of it, Wendy conceded, he had.

Despite his peculiar pyjamas.

And then, after that, they all sort of landed up in the bed. It was a big bed. Luke was already in it, Gabbie and Bruce were caught up in bedcovers and it seemed silly for Wendy to keep standing by the door when Gabbie was holding Bruce and telling Wendy to come and feel how soft his ears were... How wet his tongue was... How fat his tummy was...

So Wendy came and perched on the edge of the bed, staying as distant as she could from this pyjama-clad threat to her placidity! But then Bruce lunged at Grace. Grace toppled over in her delight at trying to reach this wonderful new toy, and Wendy had to separate them and she fell sideways...

And Grandma's bump just fitted her exactly—and there was no use resisting. So she and Luke lay side by side, and she gave in and let her sensations have their sway and chuckled at the sight of this ill-assorted brood getting to know each other.

It felt just wonderful.

But it also felt...dangerous.

What was happening? Luke was holding Grace up in the air above his head, making her chortle with pleasure. Gabbie and Bruce were somewhere under the bedclothes— good grief!—any minute now there'd be a puddle and then there'd be trouble! The bed wasn't big enough to lie too far apart, and the bumps wouldn't allow it anyway. The soft cloth of Wendy's nightgown was brushing those crazy flannelette sailing boats, and the warmth radiating out from *his* side of the bed was seductive in its charm...

'Breakfast,' Wendy said jerkily, and sat up fast. She was aware that her face was suffused with colour—which was silly. 'And that puppy needs to go outside.'

'No, he doesn't,' Luke said lazily, and grinned.

'If you don't know your puppies...' Heavens, why was the man's smile so...so darned irresistible?

'It's the very fact that I do know my puppies,' he said, still watching Wendy with that strange, enigmatic smile that had the power to make her heart do all sorts of things it had no business doing. 'Or rather, I know one puppy in particular. That puppy is very, very close to me and I also know that there's a warm, wet puddle right under my left big toe. That tells me he no longer needs to go outside at all, and I do hope we now have a working washing machine, Miss Maher.'

'We have a working washing machine.' She tried to look disapproving but it didn't quite come off. 'Right…right under your left big toe?'

'Actually right on my left big toe,' he corrected himself. He held Grace high again and grinned his gorgeous smile at his baby sister. 'And, unless I'm very much mistaken, there's a certain moistness about you, too, Grace Grey. So I believe our Wendy's right. We rise, we dry off, we have breakfast—and then we hit the day. Because there's all sorts of things I want to do today. All sorts.'

'Aren't…aren't you going back to Sydney?' Wendy managed, trying not to look as if she cared. It didn't quite come off.

'No, Wendy, I'm not,' he told her dryly. He reached under the bedclothes and retrieved Bruce, holding him high with his baby sister. One baby in one hand, one puppy in the other, and he eyed them both with misgivings. 'Rightly or wrongly, I've decided a few days spent here are in order—for me to get to know my new family. My entire new family!'

And she could make of that what she would.

An hour later, Wendy was outside hanging freshly laundered sheets over the washing line and trying to come to terms with the fact that Luke had decided to stay on. He had the right, she guessed—but she badly didn't want him to.

Why? It was important for him to get to know Grace. She knew that. Bonding was good. So what was the problem with him staying?

It was her, she thought crossly. It was the way her body responded to him. He made her feel like no one had ever made her feel before. Including Adam. Luke walked into the room and it sort of lit up.

He had the two children mesmerised—they were shrieking with laughter now as he rolled over and over on the south lawn, showing Gabbie how much faster she could roll downhill, teaching Grace to roll herself from one side to the other, and fending one puppy away from two baby noses. Gabbie, who normally held herself totally aloof, seemed besotted.

'Which I'm not,' Wendy told herself sternly. 'I can't afford to be. I'm the employee here.'

But still...

'Wendy, we need help.' Suddenly he was right beside her, handing her the next sheet, and holding one end so they could peg together.

'*We* need help? I'm the one who's doing the washing.' She glared at him. 'You didn't leave the children alone with the dog, did you?'

'Bruce is hardly going to eat them.'

'No, but—'

'And I've taught Gabbie the proper way to pick Bruce up so she won't hurt him. She really is a very intelligent little girl. You need have no qualms, ma'am. Everything is in order.'

'I—'

'And now I've helped you hang the washing,' he said virtuously. 'So it's your turn to help me. I need you.'

I need you... Three small words, but they had the power to twist her heart. Ha! Need! This man needed no one.

'What for?' She glowered with distrust but her distrust was ignored.

'The canoe's still under the house,' he told her. 'I checked. And there's life jackets. I reckon there's even one I can cut down to make a ring for Bruce. The morning's gorgeous, Miss Maher. The urgent work is done, so forget the housework. Forget responsibilities. There's places here that you've never imagined, and it'd be my very great privilege to show them to you.'

'But—'

'No argument. I'm your boss, remember.' He put a finger on her lips, and he couldn't have guessed just what sensations the touch engendered. She could hardly tell herself. 'Just come and see. And prepare to be amazed!'

She was. There was no other word for it.

Wendy had never done anything like this in her life, and she could only sit in her end of the canoe, hold on to Grace and Bruce—and wonder!

They'd launched the canoe, with Luke pulling, Wendy and Gabbie pushing and Grace and Bruce inside as they'd hauled it down across the sloping paddock to the beach. Then Luke had secured them all in assorted life jackets, had looped Wendy to Bruce and Grace—'So if you all go overboard you'll bob around together like three really weird corks until I can fish you all out'—and they'd set sail. Or set paddle if you were being picky. Which Wendy was past being.

There was hardly any need for life jackets. The day was brilliant. The water was turquoise clear; it was shallow and as calm as a millpond, and Bruce and Grace and Gabbie were so amazed they hardly moved.

They just watched. And why not? To the left of the farm, the beach gave way to a series of shallow cliffs and it was

here that Luke directed the canoe. He handled the canoe as
if he'd spent a lifetime behind the paddle—'Which I have,'
he told them. 'A childhood of paddling and permanent cal-
luses can't easily be unlearned.'

Wendy had expected just a run along the cliff line, but
to her astonishment as they neared the cliffs Luke steered
right for the rocks. Just as she was wondering what on earth
he was doing—they looked as if they'd bump hard into the
granite rock face—she saw that they were heading for an
opening.

Luke didn't pause. Catching a wave which ran them right
in, he steered inside—into an underwater cavern that had
to be seen to be believed.

It was utterly magic. Wondrous.

The first cavern was big and dark and gloomy, and
Gabbie clutched Wendy, and Wendy clutched the two babies—dog and Grace—but there was no need to worry because they were all as still as church-mice. The canoe
glided forward into the darkness—and then there was another opening...

'Oh...'

Wendy's breath was let out in a long sigh of discovery
and delight. This, too, was a cavern, but instead of being
gloomy it was lit by a hundred fissures leading up through
the rock to the brilliant sky beyond. The sun glimmered
and streamed from above, down into the shallow water. The
sea beneath them was no more than three feet or so deep,
the bottom was sandy, and a thousand little fish of every
conceivable colour flitted and darted around their boat, in
and out of the sunbeams.

'Oh...' It was all she could think of to say. She sounded
inane, but there seemed nothing else, and Luke sat back
and beamed like a genial genie who'd produced this miracle
out of a bottle.

'This is *my* cubby,' he told them proudly. 'My grandpa showed me this place when I was four years old and, as far as I know, I'm the only person in the world who knows where it is. And now I'm sharing it with you.'

He was talking to Gabbie. He must be.

But Wendy, glancing up from the wonder of the water below the boat, saw that Luke's eyes were resting on hers.

'I'm sharing it with you,' he said again, more softly, and she knew, suddenly, his words were meant for her alone.

It was like a kiss, she thought. More. It was like a declaration made right there and then, and it took her breath away. Like a fool, she blushed crimson and started to stammer.

'I...it's wonderful. Like...like a pirate's cave.'

'Full of treasure,' he said gently, and his eyes were still on hers.

Good grief! This man had seduction down to a fine art! Wendy was feeling heat rising from all sorts of places she had no idea heat could rise from. Totally bewildered, she held close the nearest object—Grace—and held her over the water. Grace's small hands reached out for the darting fish while Wendy fought wave after wave of mounting colour and emotion.

'We can beach the boat here,' Luke told them, steering the boat into the far end of the chamber where the water shallowed out to a wide stretch of soft sand. The sun glimmered down here, too—not in a steady stream but rather as individual slivers of silver, like a light show that would have cost thousands if it were man-made, but here it was done for them for free.

Up above, there were fern fronds casting their shadows over the fissures in the rocks, and the dappled light had the fronds indented into the sunbeams, and waving and shimmering in the warm sea air so the sunbeams danced and glimmered and cast a spell that was almost unbelievable in its beauty.

Wendy could hardly take it all in. She was speechless and some of the sensations she was feeling had nothing to do with this place. It had everything to do with the way this man was looking at her—the feel of his hands as he helped her out of the boat, and the way his eyes glinted down at her as if he sensed exactly what she was feeling.

Thank heaven for the children. Without them…oh, without them, who knew? But they were there. Thank heaven…

'It's…it's fantabulous,' Gabbie said, awed. At the sandy end of the cave, the chamber roof was maybe eight feet above their heads, making a comfortable and easy place to unload their boat. 'Can we paddle in the water with the fishes?'

'You can do more than paddle,' Luke told her. 'This is the very best swimming place in the world. The fish here are only tiny—the little ones seem to know it's a safe, safe place, and the water is never over your head. I persuaded Wendy to bring bathers and towels—and a picnic lunch—so the day is ours, and the magic cubby is ours and the rest of the world might well not exist.'

'You didn't bring your mobile phone?' Wendy asked and for the life of her she couldn't keep a note of bitterness from her voice, but Luke didn't appear to take offence. Not today. Not with Wendy.

'No, Miss Cynic, I did not bring my mobile phone,' he told her. 'Nor did I bring my computer. I am having a day off.'

'And yet the world will survive?' Why was she doing this?

'I hope it does,' he said gently, watching her face. 'Today's a try-out. If the world manages to get along without me today, then who knows how long I might take to get to know my family?'

'He's staying for *how long?*'

'I don't know. Weeks.' Wendy's voice was a panicking wail down the phone, and Shanni blinked. 'He's set up his office in a spare bedroom. He spends a couple of hours in there every morning but the rest of the time...'

'The rest of the time he spends with you?'

'He spends with the children,' Wendy retorted.

'Yes, but *you're* with the children.'

'I know.' Wendy tried to get a hold on herself and failed completely. Luke had been here for a week now, and she was getting more unsettled by the minute. 'This wasn't in the original agreement. Shanni, I don't know how to handle it.'

'Most nannies have to work in the same house as an employer,' Shanni said cautiously. 'It's not unreasonable for an employer to stay.'

'But he said he wasn't—'

'You think it's a bad thing for the children?' Shanni interrupted. Wendy wasn't making much sense.

'No. Of course I don't. Gabbie's in love with him. The puppy adores him. He's bonding with Grace.'

'Well, where's the problem?' Shanni said reasonably.

'I...'

'You're not falling for him yourself?'

'No. Of course not.'

'Then you just need good employee-employer guidelines,' Shanni said brightly. 'A contract. You want Nick to draw you out a nice legal agreement?'

'We have a contract.'

'Days off? Holiday pay? Employer staying at his end of the house between dusk and dawn?'

'Shanni—'

'You can't be too careful.' Shanni chortled. 'It sounds to me like this man has you badly rattled.'

'He has.' Wendy took a deep breath. 'Shanni...'

'Yes, love.' Her friend heard the worry and reacted accordingly. 'Okay. I'll be serious. Something's really worrying you?'

'He's...he's taken them all for a ride.'

Silence. Not many people would have known what this meant to Wendy, but Shanni did.

'In his sports car?'

'Mmm.'

'You're going to have to get over this, my dear,' Shanni said in her best schoolmarm voice, and her tone was almost enough to make Wendy chuckle.

'Quoth the greybeard.'

'Yes, well...' Shanni laughed too, but her concern remained. 'You need to learn to trust.'

'I know. But Gabbie—'

You need to learn to trust.

And there it was in a nutshell, Wendy thought as she replaced the phone. This was the perfect job. She should just relax and ride with the punches.

She should stop thinking Luke was trying to seduce her. She should stop thinking Luke was putting the children at risk every time he put them in the car he loved so much.

She should...trust.

She didn't. Not one bit.

'How much longer are you planning to stay?'

She shouldn't ask, but ten days had gone by and he'd shown no sign of moving. Instead, Luke seemed to be wheedling his way deeper and deeper into the running of the house, and he was doing it every way he knew how.

It was Luke who'd taken on the responsibility for Bruce's house-training—and very well Bruce was going too. He hadn't made a puddle for three days now.

It was Luke who had gone into Bay Beach and found a whole heap of easy readers—fun little books that were designed to make a child ache to read—and it was Luke who was setting himself up on the veranda each afternoon and saying 'P-U-P says pup,' and making Gabbie follow. Gabbie was so excited she could hardly leave her wonderful new books.

For Gabbie, reading seemed the most exciting thing in the world—apart from Bruce—and, watching her, Wendy had to suppress a faint twinge of jealousy at the bond that was forming between man and child.

'Join us. Help us read,' Luke often said, as he caught her watching them, but she whisked herself off back to housework that didn't need to be done or something equally trivial—because sitting beside them while they read was beguiling and bewitching and…dangerous!

It had been ten days and the tension was mounting day by day until she felt she was near to breaking point. Like now. He was so close! The children were in bed and she was washing the dinner dishes. Luke had returned after tucking Bruce into his basket and he'd picked up the tea towel and started wiping—just like an old married man. It was suddenly far too much. This unspoken intimacy that was growing stronger by the minute…

'How long do you intend staying here?' she demanded again as he failed to answer, and his brows raised in a quizzical smile.

'Am I getting under your feet, then?'

She concentrated on an infinitesimal grease spot on her frying pan, giving it her sole attention. 'Yes. A bit. I just wasn't aware that you'd ever thought of staying on.'

'I hadn't,' he said seriously. 'But things change.'

'Like what?'

And *that* was a mistake. As soon as she said it, she knew the question was a bad error of judgement—because it had to have an answer. But the question was out in the open now, like an upraised sword, with the power to bring all down around it.

And he brought it down. Finally.

'People change,' he said gently, and he laid down his tea towel and turned to face her full on. 'People like me. Two weeks ago, if you'd asked me what I thought of staying in the country, I would have told you I'd think it was purgatory—to be stuck in a farmhouse with a woman and two babies and a puppy. Now I'm starting to think it's purgatory to be anywhere else.'

'I guess...I guess that's because of Grace,' she stammered, still concentrating fiercely on her frying pan.

But suddenly the frying pan was taken out of her hands. Her wet hands were pulled to lie between his bigger ones—heavens, there were soapsuds and the soapy foam was squeezing out between their entwined fingers—and Luke was looking down into her eyes as if he was about to make a declaration.

And he did. She couldn't stop him. She desperately didn't want this, but he was saying it anyway.

'No, Wendy,' he said softly. He caught her look of startled alarm and he gave her another of his gorgeous quizzical smiles. 'I know this is way too soon. I know you're scared. So I'd really like to tell you that I've decided to stay because I've fallen in love with my little sister—as indeed I have—or because I'm falling hard for Gabbie and Bruce—and I've done that, too—but the truth is, my love, that I've fallen for you. For you, Wendy.'

'Luke—'

'You are not to look scared,' he told her sternly. He smiled down at her with such a smile that her heart lurched within her breast. 'I refuse to make you look scared. I will not rush you anywhere you don't want to go, my love. But the truth is, Wendy, that I'm falling deeper into somewhere I've never been before. I never thought I'd fall in love, but I'm totally smitten with you, and I'm prepared to hang around for however long it takes for that fear to disappear from your eyes.'

How to react to this? She tried to pull back but he wouldn't have a bar of it. His grip on her hands grew tighter.

'It never will,' she managed, and the look of blank rejection on her face made him frown.

'I'd like to know why I don't have a chance,' he said softly, and his hands were warm and strong and infinitely seductive. 'Am I so dreadful?'

'No. Yes!' She hauled back then, and he did release her, then stood watching as she turned fiercely back to her too-clean frying pan. 'You forget, I've been married before,' she told him. 'I'm not in the market for another relationship.'

'Your husband's been dead for six years,' he said, still watching her with eyes that were gently concerned. 'Does losing one love preclude any sort of relationship ever again?'

'Yes!'

'He must have been quite a man.'

'If only you knew.' She shook her head, and then, to her fury, she felt tears well up behind her eyes. Good, she thought. Let him think it was sorrow for Adam that was holding her back. 'Marriage—commitment—is something you only do once,' she managed. 'Or at least it's something I only do once. And if you keep being…ridiculous…then you'll have to find a new nanny for Grace. Gabbie and I will have to move on.'

'That's crazy.'

'It is,' she said savagely into her dishwater. 'It is indeed. To mess with a perfectly good employer-employee relationship because you want an affair...'

'It's not an affair I want, Wendy,' he said, and she cast him a startled glance. Heavens, he almost sounded as if he meant it.

'But that's all it would be,' she retorted. 'We're two completely opposite people. I'm your employee, Luke Grey, and that's the way I want to keep it. So it's that or nothing. Now, are you going to go back to Sydney—or New York—or wherever? Or not?'

He knew that much at least. 'Not,' he said decisively. 'It's occurred to me that I'm perfectly content here. Okay, you don't want me to touch you—I can live with that. For now. I promise I won't touch you unless you want. I'm a patient man. So let's get back to thinking I'm here for the children's sakes, and to get you used to me being around. For I intend to stay—for the children's sakes—for a very long time. Okay?'

'Luke—'

'It has to be okay,' he said heavily, and picked up his tea towel and started to wipe. 'It seems to me we have no choice. Either of us.'

Which was all very well, he told himself later that night, in the time when he should be sleeping. It was fine to say he had all the time in the world. In a sense, he did. He'd reorganised his job so he could work from here with only the occasional trip away. He could keep himself busy and occupied and useful.

But how could he keep his hands away from Wendy? When every single minute his body's need was deepening to a fever pitch—to a need that he'd never known in his life.

CHAPTER EIGHT

LUKE and Gabbie were halfway through a very exciting story when the car pulled up. The girl who emerged was about Wendy's age, pert and pretty. Accustomed to Gabbie bolting for cover every time a new person arrived, Luke was amazed to see Gabbie drop her book and launch herself down the veranda steps to hug the new arrival with joy.

The child was met with joy in return. Gabbie was lifted, whirled around, and then carried back to the veranda—where Shanni drooped herself into a deckchair, sighed with relief and surveyed Luke with satisfaction.

'Hi. I'm Shanni Daniels, local kindergarten teacher and friend of Wendy,' she said placidly. She put a hand down to fend off Bruce's soggy welcome. 'Down, dog. Great puppy, Gabbie, but I've already had a bath today.' She grinned at Luke. 'And I'm assuming you're Luke?'

Her smile was infectious. He smiled back. 'I'm Luke.'

'Great. Wonderful. Just don't ask me to get up and shake hands and you'll have a friend for life.' She groaned theatrically. 'Wow, this chair is good. Early pregnancy isn't all it's cut out to be. Don't even think about offering me refreshments. Unless...' Her eyes widened in hope. 'Unless you have dill pickles on hand?'

Luke grinned down at her, and joined her in the neighbouring chair, as Gabbie and Bruce whooped off cubbywards. 'Sorry, ma'am,' he told her, not without sympathy. 'Wendy's in town as we speak, doing the grocery shopping, but I can't remember that we put dill pickles on the list.'

'Then, you mustn't be pregnant. Very wise. Oh, to be a

nan.' She patted her still very flat stomach in contentment, giving the lie to her complaints, and then she directed her full attention on Luke. What she saw seemed to satisfy her. Nice,' she said.

'I beg your pardon?'

'Oh...nothing,' she said airily. 'Actually, I sort of knew Wendy was grocery shopping. I saw her in the supermarket car park and had a quick word with her. She wasn't driving the Aston Martin, I see.'

'We've bought her a wagon. She likes it better,' Luke said shortly. His smile died. 'So you knew Wendy was in town, then.'

'But yet I came on out.' Shanni's smile widened and glinted with mischief. 'I wanted to check you out while she wasn't here,' she confessed. 'You see, Wendy wasn't too keen on me visiting you.'

He blinked at that. What was Wendy playing at? Being the protective employee? 'That was good of Wendy,' he said cautiously. 'But I don't mind visitors.'

She chuckled. 'No, it wasn't good of Wendy at all. If I thought it was because she was protecting your privacy, or that she wanted to keep you all to herself, then I might have obliged and stayed away. But it was because she doesn't want me to put in my oar.'

'And do you put in your oar?' He was fascinated.

'All the time,' she confessed. 'I'm a McDonald—or I was until I met my Nick—and the McDonald girls are famous for oar-putting-in. Now, about Wendy...'

'What about Wendy?'

She looked at him closely. 'Why exactly are you staying here? Wendy said you never intended to.'

'That was before...before...'

'Before you fell in love with her?'

Luke's eyes flew wide. This was *some* conversation.

What a question! His face shuttered down in distaste, but Shanni held up her hands in entreaty.

'No, don't look like that and don't tell me to butt out,' she begged. 'I'm no good at butting out, and I'm so fond of Wendy. It's just... As I said, I met her in town and she told me you were still here and she wished you weren't— and she said you'd never intended to stay and she's so uncomfortable with your decision.'

Her keen eyes probed Luke's, asking question after question, voiced and unvoiced. 'I'm right, aren't I?' she said, and the smile was back in her voice. 'You're in love with her?'

How was he to answer a question like that? Luke sat back in his chair and stared at this amazing friend of Wendy's. Shanni stared right back, determination meeting determination. And suddenly there was nothing else to say.

'Yes,' he said simply, and he knew it then for the absolute truth. 'Of course I'm in love with her.'

'*Yes!*' She beamed, as if she'd expected no less. 'Of course you are.' She beamed some more. 'Wendy's wonderful. I can't understand why the whole world's not in love with her, but it's taken until now—until someone like you—to expose her. Well, well. How very satisfactory.'

'If you can tell me how it's satisfactory when she won't let me near—'

He got no further. 'You know she's been married?' Shanni demanded, pressing right on to what was important. She was ignoring the anger on his face. This was a totally inappropriate conversation between strangers but she seemed totally unaware of boundaries.

He might as well reply. She was going to press on regardless.

'I know that.' It was all Luke could do not to grind his

eeth at the thought of her previous marriage. 'To Adam? I gather he was perfection plus.'

'I wouldn't say that,' Shanni said cautiously.

'But—'

'But what?' Shanni's brow was wrinkling as if she was deciding what to say next.

'It's his perfection that's the problem.' Luke shook his head in despair. 'She says she's a one-man woman. Married for life. I don't stand a chance against that.'

Shanni considered this seriously. 'You don't help by being rich and handsome,' she said, thinking it through.

He blinked again. 'Pardon?'

'If Wendy could feel sorry for you, it might help.'

That was a bit much. 'Oh, great,' he said bitterly. 'That's very helpful. You'd like me to lose my fortune, get a limp or a scar or something, maybe forget a bit of personal hygiene! I'm not aiming for lame-duck sympathy here.'

It was enough. She chuckled, put her hands behind her head and surveyed him with care. 'Well, no. Maybe not. But has she told you about Adam?'

'Only that he was perfect.'

'She can't have told you that, because he wasn't,' she told him honestly. 'Adam was rich and carefree and thoughtless. He and Wendy had only been married for six months when he tried to overtake a truck in blinding rain. There was an oncoming vehicle, but he thought his gorgeous fast car had enough power to get past. He was wrong. He killed himself, he killed a baby in the oncoming car and he put Wendy in hospital for six long months.'

There was nothing to smile about there. Luke stared at Shanni in horrified disbelief. Shanni looked calmly back at him, watching his reaction. What she saw seemed to satisfy her, because she gave a brisk nod and rose.

'There. I knew she hadn't told you everything. She doesn't speak of it. The town knows that her husband died and she was badly hurt in the car crash, but they don't know Adam was responsible for the little one's death. She only told me once, and that was in a really bleak moment. It's a nightmare she can't shake off—that she feels somehow responsible herself. Because she didn't stop him.'

'Why are you telling me?'

'Because it's important,' she told him. 'And because I know my friend so well, I can tell that you're important. Or you have the capacity to be important to her. You see, Wendy's now suddenly different. There's something about you that's changed her. She's...I don't know...lit up somehow. But I know darn well she'll never let you close if she thinks you're like Adam.'

'I'm not.'

'No.'

There was just enough doubt in her voice to make his temper rise. He stood up as well and met her gaze head on, his eyes steely and cold. 'Hell, if *you* think that... If *she* thinks that...'

'If she thinks that then it's up to you to change her mind.'

'No.' He closed his eyes, and when he opened them his face was bleak. 'I can't convince her of something as basic as that. She has to know herself. It's true, I've fallen heavily for Wendy. She's...she's different. But I'm not going to be able to talk her into trusting me. She has to feel it. Like I feel it for her...'

Shanni looked at him for a long, long moment, and then she sighed. 'You're right of course,' she said sadly. 'You can't talk or manipulate someone into trusting you. You just sort of have to do it. Like me and my Nick. But still...' she brightened '...it won't hurt that you know now what you're up against.'

'I guess.'

'And there's time.' Her face broke into her smile again—persuasive and beguiling. 'Do you know it's Wendy's birthday tomorrow?'

That startled him. 'No, I didn't.'

'So a surprise is allowable,' she told him. 'What about taking the lady out to dinner?'

His brow creased. 'You mean…?'

'I mean a real dinner,' she told him. 'Wendy hasn't had a day away from her precious children for years. What about taking her somewhere really special—over-the-top special. Like Whispering Palms. That's a sweep-a-girl-off-her-feet type resort just south of the town. It would do Wendy all the good in the world for her to have a wonderful night completely free of children—and with a man like you she might just—'

'Hey, that's enough.' He smiled. 'I can make my own assumptions here.' Then he shook his head. 'She'd never leave Gabbie.'

'She would if Nick and Harry and I arrived by surprise and just took over,' Shanni said. 'Gabbie trusts me. She knows and likes Harry—our little boy—and she's met Nick. If we come out about five, bring a birthday cake to have with the kids, and then boot the pair of you out for the evening…' She looked consideringly at the house. 'We'll bring our sleeping gear and stay the night, which gives you all the time in the world.'

'To do what?'

'If you don't know then I'm not the one to be telling you,' she said demurely. 'But by the look of you your best shot might be a very good thing, Luke Grey. I'd go for it, if I were you.'

And how could he knock back an invitation like that?

*   *   *

Saturday.

All day Luke prowled like a cat on hot bricks, and by five in the afternoon Wendy was sure there was something going on. She might be keeping her distance, but she was aware enough of him to sense his moods. The man was as nervous as could be, and she didn't know why.

Or—she didn't know why until the big family station wagon pulled into the yard. Nick and Shanni and Harry were waving wildly out of the car windows and there were multicoloured helium balloons winding skyward, tied to every door handle. As the passenger door opened Wendy saw that Shanni was balancing a birthday cake that looked like...

'A Basset-hound puppy!' The cake was a near replica of Bruce's droopy cranium, complete with candle attached to the nose. It even had the same dopey expression of canine smugness.

'Because even though it's your birthday it's also a sort of welcoming party for Bruce,' Shanni explained in between laughter and introductions, birthday greetings and general mayhem. 'We even thought we might bring Darryl—that's our new kitten—but Nick thought not.'

'Nick definitely thought not,' Nick said dryly, shaking Luke's hand. 'So you're the poor soul Shanni's organising at the moment, are you? Take my advice, get out while the going's good.'

'Yeah, like you did,' Shanni jeered fondly. 'You were so scared of organisation that you married me, Nick, so don't give me that hen-pecked-husband routine. Now...' she whirled on Wendy '...has Luke told you where he's taking you this evening?'

Wendy was looking completely surprised. 'No. He hasn't.'

'Tell her where you're taking her, Luke.'

'Whispering Palms—as ordered,' Luke said, so promptly that Wendy stared.

'It's very nice,' Shanni approved. 'Isn't that nice, Nick?'

'It's the most expensive place this side of Sydney,' Nick said thoughtfully. '*Nice* is hardly a description I'd have used.'

'I'm not going to Whispering Palms,' Wendy said faintly.

'Don't be silly, love, of course you are.' Shanni grinned. 'All you need to do is blow out your birthday candles here, have a slice of cake to celebrate with the kids, and then Nick and I are going to carry on partying with your lot while you and Luke have an evening together.'

'I don't want—'

'Of course you want,' Shanni said fondly. 'Nick and I have taken a great deal of trouble to organise this. It's not every day the town's magistrate offers to baby-sit your children—even sleeping the night so it's no matter how late you get back. Now, you can wear that lovely silky apricot dress you wore to our wedding, I think.'

'Shanni!'

'This is our birthday treat,' Shanni said, in a cocker spaniel-like voice as if she expected to be kicked. Her eyes grew huge, and the faintest glimmer of a disappointed tear hung on her lashes. 'Don't say you don't want it.'

Wendy was half laughing, half close to tears herself. 'Shanni, you manipulating twerp. This is blackmail.'

'Of the very nicest kind,' Shanni said, and her twinkle returned. 'Let's get this birthday cake lit and then we'll get you two on the road. For a birthday treat to remember. For ever.'

It couldn't work.

With the help of Shanni, Luke had gone to such trouble

over this night, but almost as soon as they drove out the farm gate he knew he was headed for a disaster. He should never have let Shanni talk him into it, he thought grimly. He knew Wendy wouldn't like it.

Why not? It was the sort of evening any woman he'd ever taken out would have killed for.

For a start, the evening itself was perfect, warm and balmy and not a hint of wind with the rose-hued sunset.

Then there was the fact that personally he'd gone to some trouble. Luke was wearing his best dinner suit. It was Italian-cut and gorgeous, and he knew he looked okay in it. And Wendy... In the soft silk dress she emerged in after being prodded by Shanni, she simply took his breath away.

She'd had it made, Shanni had told him. Wendy wasn't like other women. She didn't dress for fashion, but she'd been bridesmaid at her best friend's wedding, however, so she'd done the thing in style. The dress had a high cut mandarin collar, but was open to show just the faintest hint of cleavage. It was cut with tiny crescent-moon sleeves, and was buttoned over the breast with tiny mother-of-pearl drops. The soft, swirling cloth fitted her like a glove over the hips, then flared out softly to her calves, showing every luscious curve of her gorgeous body.

It had been as much as Luke could do not to whistle as she'd emerged from the bedroom, and Nick frankly had.

Now, seated in his beautiful car, with her soft curls free and flying out behind her as they headed for the resort, she looked the most beautiful creature Luke had ever seen in his life.

But it wasn't right.

'Wendy, will you relax?' he told her. 'It's your birthday. You should be having fun.'

'I...yes.'

'The kids are safe as houses. Nick and Shanni will take the greatest care.'

'I know.'

'So what's the matter?'

She shook her head, and managed a smile. 'I don't know. Nothing. I'm being stupid. This…this is truly wonderful, Luke. A real birthday surprise.'

But it wasn't wonderful. Luke pulled the car into the Whispering Palms car park, took her hand determinedly into his and led the way into the restaurant. But he knew it wasn't wonderful at all.

It should be. This was a restaurant to dream about. The whole place had been built as a resort for millionaires. Beloved of the jet set, Whispering Palms was built as a series of tree houses set over the rainforest and the beachfront below. The walls of the restaurant swung back on balmy nights like this, so lovers could dine with the sound of the surf beneath them, with the soft wind rustling in the trees and with the ever so seductive sound of a violinist in the background…

But Wendy's face was tight with strain and, as the maître d' led them to their table Luke suddenly stopped.

'No,' he said.

The waiter paused and looked enquiringly back at them. 'Sir?'

'This isn't right,' Luke said softly, watching Wendy's face. 'I think we need some privacy.'

'A secluded table?' The man smiled his approval. 'That can be arranged.'

But Luke shook his head. Damn, he'd been a fool. He had no chance with this, and he should have known it. He should never have let Shanni talk him into it.

'That's not what I mean. Give me a moment. Wendy, wait—please.' He left Wendy standing by their allotted table, and signalled the man to move back to the reception desk. 'You're quiet tonight, aren't you?'

'Yes, sir.' The man glanced around the restaurant which was only half full.

'Then if we were to eat on the beach below…'

'Pardon?'

Luke lifted a menu and studied it briefly. 'Let me order for both of us right now,' he said. 'Then, if you can arrange it, I'd like our dinner served to us on the beach below—just around the cliff face where the river joins the sea so we're out of sight of the restaurant. I'd like full service, but after sweets and coffee then I'd like us undisturbed. You can clear the debris in the morning.'

'But sir!' The man's face had stiffened at this extraordinary request. 'I don't think…'

But Luke had opened his wallet. With a quick look back at Wendy to make sure she couldn't see, he laid down enough money to make the man stare. 'That's for the meal—so you know we won't abscond without paying—for the extra service, and there's a little more for the personal trouble you need to go to yourself. Can you arrange it?'

The man looked down at the desk where the money lay, and the corners of his mouth quirked upward in the beginnings of a smile. His mind was obviously working overtime. 'Of course I can, sir,' he said at last. 'Nothing would give me greater pleasure and, if I may say so, it's quite the most romantic notion I've ever heard of. Maybe we could start a new service…'

So, instead of being guided into one of the plush crimson seats and being handed a menu, Wendy was led back out into the night.

'This is better,' Luke said, his hand holding hers again

whether she liked it or not. 'Down these stairs, Wendy. We're going to the beach.'

'Luke—'

'Don't argue,' he said, and grinned. 'Our dinner is still being served, but served below.' He held up a lantern which had been set romantically on the reception desk but donated now to a greater cause. 'Behold our light. Lead on, my lady. Our meal awaits us.'

This was better.

The atmosphere was still strained, but it was much, much lighter than the formality of the restaurant. Wendy seemed bemused more than anything, but her sense of humour was surfacing despite her misgivings. She'd been forced into this, but it was starting to be fun.

The waiters, formally attired in black and white and not letting on by a twitch of their eyebrows that this was anything unusual, followed them down to the still sun-warmed beach which curved around the low cliffs to the river mouth fifty yards farther on. They waited patiently while Luke chose a secluded nook in the sandhills, and then they set down what they'd been carrying—a picnic rug, a candelabra, complete with candles which they proceeded to light, beautifully polished silverware, a basket of hot rolls, butter-pats, champagne glasses, champagne...

'It's like something out of a movie,' Wendy said, looking down at the magnificent spread in astonishment, and she couldn't suppress her laughter. 'For heaven's sake, of all the ostentatious...'

'It is *not* ostentatious,' Luke told her severely. 'Upstairs was ostentatious. This is a picnic.'

Wendy glanced back along the beach toward the track leading up to the restaurant. A waiter was approached bearing two silver platters. He trod solemnly across the sand to their improvised table—and she choked on her champagne as he set down the gorgeous platters before them with all the ceremony in the world. 'A picnic?'

'It sure beats sandwiches,' Luke said sagely. 'I do hope you like lobster, my dear, because this is the very best lobster that Bay Beach can produce.'

She did like lobster. She loved lobster and, despite her misgivings, she loved everything about that crazy meal. It was the dinner of dinners!—A meal to remember for ever. For the first short while she tried desperately to stay stiff and formal, but she couldn't—not while Luke kept up a patter of ridiculous banter, and the waiters came time after time, serious and steady as they trod over the sand to this amazing dining place, and carrying one magnificent dish after another.

'They think we're nuts,' she said, and Luke grinned.

'We are nuts,' he told her. 'I like it that way.' He poured more coffee from a silver jug, and offered her a plate of homemade chocolates. 'These appear to have cherries inside. Yum! Try one.'

'If I have one more thing I'll burst,' she said inelegantly. She shook her head. 'No. It's enough, Luke.' She looked back along the beach, expecting more waiters to come and clear their meal, but courtesy of Luke's forethought there was no one coming. The meal was at an end and they were alone.

Silence.

Luke's banter had died away. He was drinking his coffee and watching her in the candlelight. The soft breeze was stirring her curls around her face. The shadows made by the candlelight were dancing across her face. She looked very, very lovely.

'It's time to go home,' she said awkwardly and started to rise.

'No.' Luke set down his cup and took her hand, pulling her up beside him, like it or not. 'After a meal like that, we need exercise.'

'Oh, yeah, maybe a run along the beach,' she said a trifle breathlessly. 'You have to be kidding. I'd waddle.' She gave her hand a tug but it wasn't released. 'Luke, it's been lovely, but—'

'But the night's still young,' he told her. 'And it's warm and the beach is wonderful and our responsibilities are being taken care of. So what shall we do? I know. Let's see if we can find some prawns.'

'Prawns?'

'In case you hadn't noticed, it's a crescent moon,' he told her. 'It's the very best time for seeing prawns. Or for catching them if we had a net—or if we were hungry—but maybe we'll be content ourselves just with seeing them.'

'Where?' Despite her qualms, he had her fascinated.

'In the river,' he told her and lifted the lantern. 'We have everything we need to spot a prawn or two. Come on, Wendy Maher. Let's have fun.'

'But...'

'But what?' He fixed her with a searching look, and then smiled. 'Why are you looking like I'm about to bite? Did you think I'd set this up for a spot of seduction instead of prawn gazing? How could you?' He sounded wounded to the core and Wendy had to smile back.

'It did cross my mind,' she admitted.

'When all I wanted to do was give you a birthday treat.'

'You mean you didn't think of seduction for a minute?' Still he was holding her hand, and the thought of seduction wouldn't go away. It was right there between them, prawns or not.

He appeared to consider this seriously, but still that gentle, teasing smile remained. 'Well, I guess I could change my plans,' he said thoughtfully. 'If you really want a spot of seduction for your birthday...'

'No!'

'Then let's find prawns,' he told her. 'Damn, if I can't give you me, I'll give you a prawn or two. How's that for an alternative?'

'It seems fair enough,' she said in a voice that was none too steady. 'You or a prawn. Hmm...' She managed a chuckle but the tension between them didn't dissipate in the least. 'Let's give me a prawn any day,' she said, but she was starting to think she didn't know what she was talking about.

The choice might be easy, but the prawns themselves were hard to find. Luke led her over to the river bank. Here, where the river met the sea, the river mouth spread to a wide, sprawling network of rivulets, each no more than eighteen inches deep but, combined, stretching for a couple of hundred yards across the beach. The tide was running sluggishly outward, but it must have been close to the turn because the pools of water between the separated strands of moving tide were still.

And they were warm.

The wide, shallow river had been sun-soaked all day. Wendy slipped off her shoes, expecting cool water between her toes, but she found it was almost body temperature. Gorgeous. She stood in the shallows and watched as Luke swung his lantern slowly back and forth across the water. Again and again he swung—and the silence and the solitariness of the place made her spine tingle.

'No...no luck?' Why on earth was it hard to make her voice work?

'They must be here somewhere,' he said, as if the most important thing in the world was to find a prawn and the prawns were personally disobliging him. 'They're always here.'

'You've been prawning here before?'

'Grandpa brought me here years ago—before the resort was built.'

'Maybe they don't like tourists.'

'Prawns don't have such good taste.' He glowered into the dark. 'Where are the damned things?'

'There.' Wendy pointed a finger as a shadow crossed beneath her. 'Oh, I'm sure that's one. But it's practically translucent.'

'We need an underwater lantern,' Luke growled, trying to see what she was seeing, and the look of disgust on his face made Wendy chuckle.

'Oil lanterns and candelabra aren't all that effective underwater. Oh, there's another one. They're almost invisible.'

'Got it. No, it's gone. You're right about them being transparent. I'd forgotten.'

'It's a defense mechanism.'

'Great. And they're here to mate. How the heck do they do that?'

'Pardon?' Wendy blinked.

'They're supposed to come into the estuaries to spawn,' he said, puzzled. 'So they come when there's no moon and they're practically transparent. Now, if you were a boy prawn, looking for a girl prawn...'

'It must make it very difficult,' Wendy agreed. Still there were tingles going up and down her spine. Damn, she needed cold water here. She needed cooling down. Like her, Luke had ditched his shoes. He'd rolled up his trousers; he was standing knee-deep in the water in his gorgeous dinner jacket and bow tie, and the lantern was playing light beams over his face. Now he was staring intently into the water, talking of girl prawns and boy prawns. And suddenly it was as if the sand was shifting under Wendy's feet. Leaving her dizzy...

'How do you think he'd find her—the boy prawn and the girl prawn, I mean?' Luke was asking, and she concentrated fiercely on being sensible. On not being dizzy.

'Maybe they just bump into each other in the dark,' she said unsteadily. 'And cling.'

'It might work,' he agreed, still staring down into the water. 'But it shows a sad lack of discrimination on the part of the individual prawns. What if the boy prawn named Jake specifically wants a girl prawn called Maud?'

'She'd have to wear a distinctive perfume,' Wendy ventured. 'I don't know what, though. Eau-de-fish or something?'

'So then he'd be able to find her?' Luke said thoughtfully, turning his attention from prawn-hunting to the girl by his side. 'In the dark?'

'If...he wanted her badly enough.' Why? Why was she breathless?

'He does.' Luke took a deep breath and seemed to come to a decision. He raised his lantern, and turned the wick down. The light flickered off. Then, deliberately, he walked back to the shore, set his lantern down on the dry sand and splashed back to her. The look in his eyes was different now. As if a decision had been made, and there was no going back.

And Wendy could hardly breathe...

'He wants her very badly indeed,' Luke said, and he lifted a hand to run his fingers through her curls. 'So badly he can hardly bear it.'

'Are we...?' Good grief, how to make herself breathe in and out? He was so close. This was so...inevitable. So right...

It must be the champagne, she told herself desperately, ut she knew it was no such thing. 'Are we talking about rawns here, Luke Grey?'

'We were,' he said softly, and his hand lifted her hair nd twisted it away from her face. There was so little ght—just a sliver of silver from the crescent moon—but : was enough for him to see what he needed. His Wendy. is love. 'We've moved on,' he told her.

'Luke…'

'No.' He touched her lips, ever so lightly with his fingers. You are *not* to internalise here. You're not to think "what f?" What if I'm like Adam? What if this doesn't work ut? What even of tomorrow? For now…for now, I want ou to tell me what you're feeling. Right now.'

'I can't.' It was as if she was frozen solid, standing still n the shallows while his hands sent currents of fire right hrough her entire body.

'Then I'll tell you what I'm feeling,' he answered. His ands cupped her face, forcing her to meet his eyes. 'I'm eeling just like our prawn, Jake, who's probably zooming round our ankles as we speak, desperately searching for is lady love. Only I've found mine. And you know the tupid thing? It seems I've been searching all my life, and didn't even know I was searching until I found her.'

'No!'

'Let me speak,' he said forcibly, so forcibly that her eyes widened in shock. 'I've taken a great deal of trouble to ave you standing here, and the least you can do is listen or a bit. It's common courtesy.'

This unlover-like speech made her blink, but she was a girl of spirit. 'It's my birthday,' she said with asperity. 'If . don't want to listen to speeches on my birthday I don't ave to.'

'It's eleven forty-five. If we're quibbling then we'll wait

for another fifteen minutes until it's not your birthday.' He gripped her hands, like it or not, and went right on where he'd left off. 'Wendy, I never thought I would fall in love—'

'Love!'

'Shut up,' he told her kindly. 'Yes. Love. You know what it is. I know what it is. It's what's between us.'

'It's not!'

'Don't quibble,' he ordered. 'I just have to look at the way you react to me to know you feel this. This...bond. Like we're two halves of a whole and we're not right unless we're together. I've spent the last ten years or so searching for the most beautiful woman. The wittiest. The most influential. I've gone out with one beautiful dingbat or intellectual wit after another.'

'I don't need to hear about your past love life,' she said faintly, trying unsuccessfully to drag her hands away.

'Yes, you do,' he said, and his voice was suddenly savage. 'Like I need to know about Adam. We need to acknowledge it and then move on. Because it's different. What's between us is so different it's like we've been transported to another life. I want you, Wendy. I need you. I want to marry you, live with you, cherish you. Have more babies with you. Buy a few more puppies, even. But most of all...'

She was powerless to say a word. She could only listen.

His eyes gleamed down at her in the silvering moonlight. 'Most of all,' he said softly. 'Right now...right now all I want is to make love to you. I want to take you to me and hold you and feel the warmth of your body, and I want it before you have time for any of your precious qualms. I love you so much, my beautiful Wendy, and I can't see how you can stand here and not feel this thing I'm feeling...'

'Luke, stop,' she begged. 'I can't.'

'You can't?' He smiled down at her, so tenderly that she thought she must surely melt into him. 'You can't? You didn't say: you don't.'

'I...'

'Can you say it, my love? Can you look at me and say, "I don't love you"?'

She must! But Luke's hands were holding hers, he was drawing her in so her breasts were moulding to his chest, and what she was feeling...

She'd never felt like this, she thought wildly. Not with Adam. With no one.

And Luke was looking down at her, then his face was buried in her hair, and she could feel his breath warm on her skin and his heart was beating in time with hers. They were still standing knee-deep in the warm outgoing tide; the night was black velvet around them and there was no room for anything but the truth.

Don't think of tomorrow...

There was only this night. This night and then...nothing?

There'd been nothing for ever, she thought bleakly. Since Adam's death there'd been nothing, or even before that, when she knew she'd made such a mistake with her marriage. And now...safe in this man's arms, with his hold on her tightening by the minute. It was so sweet... So seductive...

Don't think of tomorrow...

She lifted her face, just a little, but it was enough.

'Let me love you, Wendy,' he said in a voice that was none too steady. 'Let me love you, my love. Now and for ever.'

And who could resist? A girl would have to be less than human to resist.

She closed her eyes, and when she opened then the decision had been taken out of her hands. Luke was kissing her, so deeply she thought she'd drown. His hands were claiming her and she was being lifted into his arms and carried back to the waiting sandhills.

And she knew, whatever came tomorrow, for now there was only this night, this man...

And joy.

CHAPTER NINE

AWN.

As the sun slipped over the horizon, Luke stirred with
Wendy in his arms. He held her close, savouring this last,
long moment of wonder, and then he kissed the nape of
her neck to make her stir. Needs must...

'Love?'

She woke, wondering, and, as she saw that it was daylight her eyes flew wide in panic. 'No!'

'It's fine.' His grip tightened. He wasn't letting her go
for the world, but it said a lot for his instinctive understanding of this woman that he knew what her first thought
would be. Her children. 'Nick and Shanni are staying at
the farm for the night. You knew that. They're not expecting us back until breakfast.'

She thought about this, panic subsiding. She grimaced—
but then it was hard to grimace very much when she was
feeling so light and so loved and so incredibly wonderful.

'I've been set up,' she said, and he chuckled.

'You have. But soon...' he glanced at his watch '...soon
the staff from the resort above will come down and clear
the remnants of last night's debauchery, and we're not exactly in a position to receive them.'

They weren't. She blushed bright crimson at that. Good
grief! If anyone had ever told her she'd sleep naked on a
beach, wrapped only in a picnic rug, and not very securely
at that...

'A swim and dress, I think,' Luke said ruefully. 'Before
we have visitors. What do you think, my love?'

157

What did she think? There was only one thing sh[e]
wanted to do more than swim. But Luke was right, the[y]
had to be sensible—or a little bit sensible.

So she didn't argue—and who could argue when he wa[s]
lifting her and carrying her across to the river which wa[s]
now deep and cool and wonderful with the incoming tide—
and he was lowering her down into the water and she wa[s]
gasping and laughing and holding him and devouring hi[s]
wonderful body with her eyes.

And she was so far in love that she felt she could floa[t]
not just in the water but anywhere. As long as Luke wa[s]
beside her.

But...

This was tomorrow.

It was okay for a start. It was fine, even. Dressed—after [a]
fashion, though they did look a whole lot less respectabl[e]
than the two gorgeous diners who'd entered the restaurar[t]
the night before—they crept hand in hand up the track[,]
skirted the resort buildings and made their getaway withou[t]
sighting anyone.

'Great.' Luke grinned as he nosed his lovely little ca[r]
out onto the highway. He looked across at his love and hi[s]
grin intensified. 'Though if we'd been seen they neve[r]
would have recognised us from last night. You look like [a]
mermaid, my love.'

'You mean there's seaweed in my hair.' She lifted [a]
strand of sea-soaked curls and regarded it ruefully. 'Just a[s]
long as we can sneak inside at the other end.'

'It's still before seven. We have every chance.'

'We have children and puppies,' Wendy said. 'We hav[e]
no chance at all. Nick and Shanni will jump to all sorts o[f]
conclusions.'

'Let them.' Luke glanced sideways at her again, and the[n]

look on his face made her warm from the toes up. 'They'll all be right. Unless they figure we're already married and even that—'

'Luke...' She faltered.

'Yes, love?'

'You're going too fast.'

He eased off the accelerator and she gave a sideways smile. 'I didn't mean that.'

'What do you mean?'

'I mean...marriage.'

'It's what I want,' he said steadily. 'I want you, Wendy. For ever. Can you handle that?'

'I don't know.'

'You knew last night.'

'Yes, but...' She faltered again and shook her head. 'Luke, it's happened so fast. I met Adam and married him fast, and it was such a mistake.'

His brow darkened. 'I'm not Adam.'

'No, but...'

'But what?'

She stared across at him for a long, long minute, trouble written on her face. Then...

'Will you sell this car?' she burst out.

Silence.

Would he sell this car? Luke faced the road again, and unconsciously his foot pressed more firmly on the accelerator. Sell...

He didn't love this car, he acknowledged, frowning into the silence. Not like he loved Wendy and the kids. But...

'Why do you want me to sell it?'

'Because it's foolish.'

'Because it's like Adam?'

'Yes,' she burst out before she could stop herself. 'To have a car that's so powerful is so stupid!'

'It's not a stupid car, Wendy,' he said carefully. 'It's a beautiful car. Sure, it's expensive, but it's a craftsman-made piece of engineering that gives me real pleasure. I have never used it unwisely. I have never driven faster than is safe, and I've never been stupid in it. But if you think that me owning it makes me like Adam...'

'I'm sorry, but—'

'I'm not like Adam,' he told her, the frown still in his voice. 'I'm *me*. And what else will you want me to do if we go down that road? Get rid of any suits that might make me look like Adam? Sleep on the other side of the bed to the one he did? Eat different brands of toast spread?'

'It's ridiculous, I know—'

'It *is* ridiculous,' he said. 'It's also insulting. You have to know that I'm different. I'm asking you to marry me, Wendy. *I* am asking you. But if you think for one minute that I'm like Adam then I don't want a bar of it. So no, I won't sell this car. Not because I can't, or because I'm more attached to it than I am to you, but because it's part of who I am. The whole package. Futures broker, nice car, leather jackets... If you want commitment then you need to love me for *me*, Wendy, or you don't love me at all.'

And that was that.

What was he saying? he thought bleakly. Luke sat back and clenched his hands on the steering wheel until white bone showed through his knuckles. Had he thrown away his best shot here?

But somewhere in the back of his brain, he knew he was right. He loved this woman beside him with all his heart, but he couldn't spend the rest of his life marching behind Adam's ghost. Always making sure he wasn't reminding her...

'Luke—'

'It's your decision, Wendy,' he said grimly.

'I just...' And then her eyes widened and her voice changed to panic. *'Luke!'*

He'd seen it. The wombat was sitting right in the middle of the road as they rounded a blind curve. Sleek and black and fat, it sat immovable as a rock.

Luke hit the brakes with everything he had. The car veered sideways onto the verge, tyres screaming. The whole vehicle lifted as it hit the gravel, it tottered for one endless moment as though trying to decide whether to go over—and then it settled again blessedly onto four steady wheels.

Luke and Wendy were left staring straight ahead as the car came to a skidding halt, with Luke blessing brilliant braking systems and fabulous stability—and just a little bit of luck thrown in for good measure.

Whew! They hadn't even hurt the wombat!

'Are you okay?' He looked across at Wendy and she was as white as a sheet. She'd closed her eyes, and her whole body was trembling. 'Hey, it's okay, love,' he said gently. 'We didn't hit it.'

'We could have.' Her voice was hardly a whisper. 'Luke, it could have been a child.'

'We didn't and it wasn't.' He gave her a worried glance, but if she was uninjured he had other urgent priorities. Another car might come around the curve at any minute and the stupid great creature hadn't moved. He sighed and lifted his travel rug from the back seat. Wombats weighed a ton, but another glance at Wendy's white face told him he was on his own.

Five minutes later, with one wombat safely carried a couple of hundred yards into the bush—over a creek-bed so it couldn't easily get back again—and given a solid lecture about road safety, he returned to the car to find Wendy still staring straight ahead and her pale face white with strain.

It had brought back the accident from all those years ago he thought. Hell! This was just what he didn't need.

'Wendy, we're fine,' he told her. 'The wombat's fine too, not that it deserves to be.'

'It mightn't have been.'

'It is.'

'It's this car,' she whispered, and that brought him up short.

He wheeled to face her, putting his hands out to grasp her shoulders and forcing her around so she had to meet his eyes. There was anger blazing in his face—hell, he'd had a shock, too, and to blame this car…

'No, Wendy, it was *not* this car,' he told her. 'We were going at a sensible speed on a country road. Yes, sure if I'd had a four-wheel drive vehicle with a bullbar in front *we* might have gone straight over the top of the wombat without any damage, but we would have killed it. And if we'd hit him in a nice, sensible station wagon—a lump like that weighing half a ton—then we may very well have overturned and been hurt.'

'We were going too fast.'

'You mean—*I* was going too fast.'

'Yes.'

'I was going at far less than the speed limit,' he said icily. 'Will you get it into your head that I'm *not* Adam?'

But she was past logical thought. 'If we'd hit him—if we'd gone over and been killed—Grace and Gabbie would be alone.'

'Wendy—'

'I should never have come,' she said, and her hands went up to her face in horror. 'Of all the crazy, irresponsible things to do… I'm all Gabbie has, Luke.' She took a deep, searing breath, searching for steadiness, and with it came some measure of calm. But also determination. 'Take me home, please,' she said, and by the sound of her voice there was no argument possible. 'I've been really, really stupid. I've been a fool for the second time, and it has to be the last.'

And that was that.

Wendy was immovable. Solid as a rock. Luke took her home; she disappeared to her end of the house without saying a word and he didn't see her again until everyone was seated at the breakfast table. By then she had her face nicely under control again. She was briskly, kindly formal, and Luke had been put onto another planet. One where she didn't exist.

'Are you two going to tell us you had a nice time?' Shanni asked doubtfully, looking from one face to the other. She'd had such hopes of last night, and then when they hadn't come home...

'We had a nice time,' Wendy told her, trying to smile. 'We went prawning, but we didn't catch anything.'

And you didn't even catch each other, Shanni thought sadly, exchanging a meaningful glance with Nick. Oh, dear. They'd given their best, but it wasn't enough.

'We'll be off, then,' she said doubtfully. 'But call us again. Any time you want us to baby-sit...'

'We don't need you,' Wendy said, concentrating fiercely on her toast. 'What you did was lovely—thank you both very much—but Luke will be returning to the city soon, and I won't be leaving the children.'

'Will you really be returning to Sydney?' Shanni asked, and watched Luke's strained face.

He shook his head. 'I haven't decided but...' he shrugged '...maybe it's just as well if I don't stay much longer.'

And maybe it was.

*   *   *

For the next two days Luke tried to keep things as they'd been but it was impossible. The strain between the two of them was almost unbearable—so much so that Gabbie asked, 'Why does Wendy always look like she's going to cry after you go out of the room?'

Luke couldn't answer, but he knew. Of course he knew. It was because Wendy had fallen as deeply in love with him as he had with her—but how to say that to a child? And how to expect Gabbie to understand why Wendy wouldn't let things ride to their inevitable, joyous conclusion when he hardly understood her reasons himself?

'You want me as much as I want you,' he said to her on the second evening after their night out, when the children were safely in bed. He'd come out to find her on the veranda and had discovered her staring out to sea with eyes that were bleak and despairing. 'How can you deny it?'

She looked at him with eyes that defeated him with their misery. 'I might want you but I know where that wanting has led in the past,' she whispered. 'Luke, please...don't do this to me. It's tearing me in two.'

'And it's not tearing me?'

'You'll get over it,' she said drearily. 'Don't tell me there won't be other women.' She wheeled to face him. 'Oh, for heaven's sake, just leave it. Can't you see I don't want a relationship? I was utterly mad to let myself imagine I could love you. To let you make love to me. One night's madness...'

'No,' he said softly. 'One night's honesty and one night's joy. One night's beginning of the rest of our lives. I don't do casual sex, Wendy. I made love to the woman I want to marry—with the woman I wish to spend the rest of my life with—and I'm damned sure under that bleak exterior that that's what you want, too.'

'I don't want it, Luke,' she said again. 'And as for letting down my defences… It's not going to happen again. No matter how long you stay here. You're my employer. You have the cutest baby in the world. I'm desperate to stay here and stay looking after her, but I've told you before that if you keep this pressure on then I'll have to go. Gabbie and I will move on.'

She would too. He looked at her despairingly but there was nothing in her face but resolution and misery. He was making her unhappy, he thought suddenly. Hell, he loved her and he was making her unhappy!

'You really want me to go?' he asked, and watched the flare of hope behind her eyes.

'This is your home. You own it. I can't force you to leave.'

'But you want me to?'

'Luke, I can't take this pressure,' she said honestly, and she spread her hands in appeal.

'Because you love me?'

'I…can't.'

'And yet you do.' He didn't touch her. He didn't move. They were standing four feet apart and he knew if he took one step nearer then she'd turn and leave.

'I told you,' she said steadily. 'I can't.'

'Hell!'

'It is,' she said bleakly. 'A very special sort of hell.'

'Because you can't trust again.'

'I'm all Gabbie has,' she said simply.

'You don't think by loving me that Gabbie could have both of us? Grace could have both of us? That the responsibility and the love could be shared? You wouldn't be all Gabbie has. She'd be a part of a family.'

'Luke—don't.'

He closed his eyes. How to make her trust? How?

He couldn't. Selling his car, changing his clothes—they

were just the superficial things. This was a deeper fear, and hoping that she'd change was like hoping for the moon. So face it, he told himself harshly. To drag this out was killing both of them.

'Okay, Wendy,' he said, and his voice was flat with defeat. 'You've got your way. I'll leave in the morning.'

'Oh, Luke…'

'It's what you want, isn't it?'

There was only one answer to that. There had to be. She tilted her chin and forced herself to meet his eyes. 'Yes.'

'Then, that's that, then,' he told her. 'That's that. Until you can find the courage to trust your heart…'

'My heart leads me to nothing but trouble.'

'That's funny…' he said, but there was nothing funny in the way he said it '…because my heart's leading me to nothing but joy. Until it comes face to face with your damned barriers, with your mistrust, and it's learning for the first time just how hurtful that can be. I'll leave, Wendy. And I hope you can be happy with that decision, because I sure as hell can't.'

'We must be,' Wendy managed.

'Give me one good reason.' He sighed and shrugged his shoulders, anger building. 'You can't and neither can I. This is just plain stupid, but it's up to you to get over it.'

CHAPTER TEN

'YOU'VE sent him away!'

'He left. I didn't send him. If he'd wanted to stay then he could have. It's his house after all.'

'But it was you who wanted him to go.' Shanni blazed indignation. 'You are out of your cotton-picking mind! Of all the stupid, crazy... Wendy Maher, that man is seriously in love with you.'

'Yes.'

The flat reply was enough to make Shanni blink. *You mean you know?* Shanni was almost speechless. 'Wendy, what is wrong with you? He's gorgeous, he's rich, he's kind. He has the most beautiful baby sister. Gabbie's half in love with him already, he owns this place, *and he loves you...*'

'I don't trust him.'

That set Shanni back. She'd driven out the day after Luke had left to find her friend staring sightlessly at Gabbie playing on the beach while Grace napped on a rug beside her. She'd never seen this look on her friend's face, Shanni thought, and she couldn't understand it. She looked desolate.

'So what's he done to make you mistrust him?'

'I don't know.' Wendy closed her eyes and dug her fingers into her palms. 'Nothing. Just been Luke.'

'And that's something to mistrust?'

'He still drives that car.'

'Oh, great. The man has an expensive car.'

'It's not entirely that.' Wendy sighed helplessly. 'How

167

to make you see? It's not just the car. Or the fact that he's wealthy. It's…it's how he makes me feel. Like I'm out of control.'

'Because you're in love with him.'

'Yes. *No!* I don't know.'

'You are,' Shanni said, satisfied. 'And you don't like being not in control. You don't like placing your trust— your heart—in someone else's hands.'

'I have no right to risk the children…'

'Now, by saying that then you're just being silly,' Shanni said flatly. 'You are my very dearest friend and I hate to say this but in sending Luke away you are acting like you're a sandwich short of a picnic.'

Wendy looked at her, her eyes troubled. 'That's what Luke thinks.'

'So he knows you're in love with him?'

Wendy thought back to their night of lovemaking at the beach and despite herself her mouth twitched into the beginnings of a smile. 'He might have guessed.'

'I knew our baby-sitting wasn't all in vain.' Shanni sat back and hugged her knees. 'How very satisfactory. So we've established that Luke loves Wendy and Wendy loves Luke. Now all we have to do is bang two thick heads together and make them see sense.'

'Shanni, I am *not* remarrying.' Grace stirred on her rug, and Wendy stooped to lift her into her arms and hug her. It was almost a defensive action. See me, her gesture said, I have my children. What else could I want? 'I've been down that road before,' she said drearily into Grace's soft curls. 'I am not travelling it again.'

'*He's asked you to marry him?*' Shanni's voice was an excited squeak. 'He's *that* in love?'

'I told you—'

'You've told me nothing that makes sense.' Shanni stood

up and glared. 'You've been down some dangerous and eventually disastrous road with Adam, but this is Luke, Wendy. He's a darling. Give the man some credit for being different.'

'Shanni, leave it.'

'You'll be making him desperately unhappy. Does he deserve that?'

'He'll get over it.'

'Will he?' Shanni's eyes narrowed. 'If he's as much in love as I think he is, he may never get over it.'

He hadn't got over it. Not then, and not two months later.

Sure, he tried to fit back into his old life but it wasn't what it was. Mostly because every waking minute his thoughts would flit to what would be happening at the farm. What would be happening with Wendy.

He rang once a week, from wherever he was in the world which was as far away as he could make it. He figured it was easier being in New York than Sydney—then he knew he couldn't just get in the car and drive and be with them in hours. The temptation would be irresistible. So New York—and London and Paris—became desirable places to be and he threw himself into his work harder than he'd ever done in his life before.

Half a world away, Wendy and the kids seemed as if they were doing the same.

His weekly phone calls told him the facts, told in a formal employee to employer tone from Wendy. The house was being totally repainted inside and out. Gabbie had started school and was loving it. Grace had cut her first tooth...

The facts were recounted in a much more bouncy, excited way by Gabbie when Wendy handed the phone over—with a sigh of relief that made Luke feel ill. He had to haul himself together to respond to Gabbie.

She took some responding to, and more and more his heart went out to her. The cow in the next paddock had had a calf and Gabbie had watched. Bruce could sit for a whole count to ten, and Grace had sucked Bruce's tail and Bruce had liked it so much he'd kept sitting beside her and wagging his tail in her face so she'd do it some more…

It made him so homesick he wanted to slam the phone back on the receiver in disgust, but he held on, soaking up every ounce of the contact that he could. And then he took his bad temper out on the futures market, and his fortune increased like it never had before because he personally was so angry he had to take it out some way. On something…

And his secretary tiptoed around him and watched him with eyes that were concerned. The middle-aged lady liked her boss, and she wasn't stupid. She could guess what was doing this, but there was nothing she could do to help. So she protected him as much as she could and worried in private until…

The phone call came mid-morning New York time, and it wasn't the normal sort of business call Luke received. The lady on the end sounded young and distressed and a little…desperate?

'Is this the right number for Luke Grey—the Australian share broker?'

'Futures broker,' Maria corrected gently, and then softened. 'Yes, dear, it is.'

'This is Shanni Daniels. I'm…I'm a friend of a friend of Luke's. The…the mutual friend is in trouble and I really, really need to speak to him.'

Maria thought of her boss, up to his ears in paperwork

and she thought of her instructions. 'Don't put anyone through until after lunch. No one, Maria. Is that clear?'

It was perfectly clear. But... 'Are you ringing from Australia?' she asked, and couldn't quite keep the note of hope from her voice.

'That's right.' Shanni's breath came out in a rush. 'I hope the time isn't too awful over there. I waited until really late. Nick says it's none of my business, but, please, it's really important.'

'Is the mutual friend a lady?'

Silence. And then, 'Yes,' Shanni said flatly. 'Yes, she is.'

'I'm putting you through now, dear,' Maria said calmly and flicked the switch.

Hell, this column didn't make sense. He'd entered the figures into his spreadsheet three times and it wasn't working. This is moron stuff, Luke told himself. Get a grip, Grey.

And then the phone went and he glared at it as if it was his personal enemy. He'd told Maria he wasn't to be disturbed...

'Maria!' he roared.

No answer.

Balked, he stalked over to the door and flung it open. Maria's desk was empty. She must have gone to the bathroom and switched the phone through to his office first—which wasn't like her.

So let it ring!

The figures still wouldn't add up...

The phone kept ringing.

Finally, he lifted the receiver and yelled, as if it was Maria he was yelling at. *'What?'*

'Luke?' The voice at the end of the line was so faint that he didn't recognise it.

'Yes?' He lowered his tone a notch—but not so much that you'd notice.

'It's Shanni. You know, Wendy's friend.'

'Oh, God.' Half a world away from her, his heart lurched into his boots and stayed. 'What's wrong?'

'It's Gabbie,' she told him. 'Luke, I thought you needed to know. Gabbie's mother's coming to take her away again.'

Gabbie's mother's coming to take her away... Luke's mind went blank, fiercely rejecting what he'd just heard. No!

He couldn't bear it, he thought, and it was a measure of his love for his whole new little family that his thoughts went first not to Wendy but to Gabbie. After what Wendy had said about her mother, to have her dragged away...

And after that, how must Wendy be feeling? Watching the child she loved being taken away to horror...

'Can anyone do anything about it?' Did he sound as sick as he felt?

'Tom says not.' His sickness was matched in Shanni's tone. 'Tom's the head of the Home system here, and he's feeling as bad as everyone about it, but she's been through the courts. It's supervised—our workers will be able to go in and check, but her cruelty in the past has been...not the kind that gets a kid taken away.'

'Hell.'

'Yes.' Shanni's bleakness reached him down the phone and he thought if this woman was feeling bad, how much more so must Wendy be feeling?

'Does her mother really want Gabbie?' he asked.

'Wendy still thinks it's a power thing,' Shanni told him. 'Sonia never tries to make any contact, but then she gets bored and angry and she feels like getting her own back on life, so she moves in on her daughter. If she knew Gabbie was living at the farm in almost permanent care...'

'She doesn't know that?'

'No, and she mustn't. Wendy's bringing her into the Home office on Wednesday morning, so as far as Sonia knows she's still living in a foster home. Otherwise Wendy will never get her back. Sonia will see to that. Oh, but Luke...'

There was worse to come. He could hear it.

'Yes?'

'Sonia's talking about taking Gabbie to Perth—in Western Australia.'

'What does that mean?'

'It means if she's placed in foster care again she'll go into the Western Australian system. Wendy... Wendy won't get her back.'

More silence. Luke's mind, which had stalled into a dead halt, suddenly started up in overdrive.

'Wednesday morning, you say?'

'That's right.'

It was Monday evening Australian time now. That gave him thirty-six hours.

'Can you get me this—who did you say was in charge?—Tom's home phone number?'

'I...'

'Do it, Shanni,' he told her. 'I'd imagine Erin will have it. Don't tell Wendy, but let's see if we can start some wheels spinning. I may not be able to help but—'

'But you'll try?'

'With everything I have,' he said, and he meant it.

He just wished he had more.

It was a bleak little ceremony. How could it be anything else? Wendy wondered. For most of the kids she'd cared for, a parent coming to claim them was a time of joy. For Gabbie, it meant a white face, fiercely expressionless eyes and a hand that clung to Wendy's as if she was drowning. Her bag was packed, she was staring across the Home administration's front desk at her mother, and her fingers pleaded with Wendy to keep her more than she'd ever wanted anything in her life.

But Wendy had to let her go.

'Do you regard this as a long-term arrangement?' Tom was asking Sonia Rolands. Tom Burrows, the head of Social Services for the district, was in his sixties, he'd been in this game for a long, long time but even he wasn't case-hardened against Gabbie's appalled face.

'It might be,' Sonia said airily. 'I've met this new bloke over in Perth. We thought we might, you know, have a shot at a new life. The kid can come with us for a while and we'll see how it goes. He thinks he might like a kid.'

You mean you can disrupt your child's life with little bother to you, Wendy thought grimly. The woman had hardly even acknowledged Gabbie's presence. She'd simply walked into the office and waited for the handover.

'Wouldn't it be better for you to settle into living over there first?' Wendy suggested quietly. 'Find a place to live, settle with your new man and have us send Gabbie to you then?' She took a deep breath. 'I'd cover the plane fare.'

The woman cast her a hard and suspicious glare. 'What business is it of yours?'

Uh-oh. That had been a mistake, Wendy thought. She mustn't let this woman see that she cared. 'Children's services has money for such contingencies.' She forced her voice carefully into neutral. 'We like to see our families settled with every possible chance of making a go of it.'

'Yeah, well, the only thing that'd help me is a new car.' The woman gave a hard, shrill laugh, and motioned out the window to where her ancient sedan stood in the driveway. 'If you have any spare cash floating around you can donate it to that. You see that getting over the Nullarbor? The kid'll have to get out and push.'

And she wouldn't put it past her to make her, Wendy thought wearily but, as Tom shook his head, she carefully disengaged those clutching fingers and gave Gabbie a gentle push toward her mother. The law was the law and Wendy had no rights here at all. 'Your mummy's waiting, Gabbie,' she said.

'Gabbie's been given a pup,' Tom ventured, still caught by Gabbie's appalled face. 'She's become very attached. How do you feel about taking him, too?'

'A dog!' Sonia's eyes widened. 'You have to be joking? What the hell would I do with a dog?'

'Mummy...' Gabbie ventured her own whispered plea. 'Mummy, I really love Bruce.'

That was enough. Sonia's eyes turned to flint. 'All the better to leave it here now,' she said flatly. 'There's no way I'm taking a dog anywhere and I'm not getting rid of any dog. Unless I dump it at the first corner. You lot do it.' She grabbed Gabbie's hand. 'That's all your stuff in the bag? Good! Then, that's all I'm taking. Say goodbye, kid. With luck, you'll never see these people again.'

With luck...

It was too much. Wendy was practically choking, trying to hold back her tears, and even Tom looked sick. Wendy turned away, and then she paused.

There were cars turning into the drive. Three cars. Who? They stopped one after another and doors opened.

Nick emerged first from his station wagon. What was Nick doing here?

A sleek black Mercedes arrived next with two men in the front seat.

And last was Luke's Aston Martin…

They were certainly here on business. Stunned, Wendy watched as the men congregated, greeted each other and strode purposefully to the front door. They were all business-suited and they came straight in—as if they were expected—and she whirled around to find Tom's sick look had changed to an expression of vast relief.

'What…?'

But Tom wasn't listening. 'If you'd wait a moment, Mrs Rolands,' Tom said as the four men entered. 'These people have a proposition to put to you.'

'A proposition?' Sonia stared. 'I don't want no—'

'Are you Mrs Rolands?' It was Luke. He'd entered first, had cast one sweeping glance around the office, had taken in Wendy's distress, Gabbie's fear, Tom's relief—and now he concentrated solely on the woman on the other side of the table. He laid down a folder and opened it wide. 'I'm very sorry we're late. You'll understand we had a lot of organisation to do since we heard you were coming for Gabbie, and I've only just flown in from New York.'

'New York? Who the hell are you?'

'I'm Luke Grey.' They might have been alone in the room together—he and Sonia. This was Luke at his businesslike best, and he was letting nothing stand in his way of his intentions. 'I employ Miss Maher, here.' He motioned to Wendy but he carefully didn't meet her eyes. There was no way personal involvement could be hinted at. 'I employ her to look after my half-sister. I'm an international businessman, and I don't have time to care for the child myself. The pressures of work, you understand.' He gave Sonia a brief but not unsympathetic smile. His wheedling smile. 'I'm sure as a single mother you must feel the same.'

'I…yes.' Sonia was flummoxed.

'The thing is that my small sister has taken a fondness to your Gabbie.' He made no mention here that Grace was seven months old and took a liking to everyone. 'As you may know, in her role as Home parent, Miss Maher has been looking after your child, too. I'm here to see if we can work out a way for that arrangement to continue—for the children to remain together long-term.'

Sonia's eyes narrowed in distrust. 'The kid comes with me.'

Luke nodded. 'I can understand that as a mother you'd be very distraught to give your child up. But Mr Burrows, here...' he motioned to Tom '...has indicated you've thought of adoption before. You've signed pre-adoption papers and then pulled out at the last moment—like you are now.'

'I might have.' Still the hard suspicion. 'What of it? I can change my mind any time I want.'

'But seeing you've left your child in care for the requisite few months before adoption can be finalised, and you've done this a number of times now, I wondered,' Luke said smoothly, 'whether there may be some way we could make your final decision easier.'

'Such as...'

'Such as cash, for instance?'

'We're not in the market of selling children,' Tom said quickly, and Luke gave him a brief nod.

'I understand that.' He motioned to the men behind him—three of the solidest looking men you were ever likely to meet. 'These men are all qualified lawyers. Nick here is Bay Beach's local magistrate, Charles is my personal lawyer and David is specialised in family law matters. They've explained to me that no pre-adoption payment is acceptable. But Gabbie has been placed under foster care pre-adoptively on a number of occasions. If Mrs Rolands

relinquishes her now, an offer making things easier for he
in the future could be considered reasonable. It would be a
personal matter between the two parties, with no bearing
on the adoption.'

'An offer? How much?' He'd caught her now. The
woman was staring at Luke as if he was holding the Holy
Grail. Money…

'Say…two-hundred-thousand dollars?' Without further
hesitation he lifted a cheque from his breast pocket and laid
it on the table. The piece of paper fluttered toward her, and
her eyes turned to it, riveted.

'You've got to be kidding. Two hundred grand…'

'I'm not kidding, Mrs Rolands,' Luke said gently. 'My
half-sister needs a companion and I want her to have
Gabbie.'

'You're crazy.'

'Maybe. But it's a once only offer. If you take Gabbie
away now, my sister may become attached to another child
and I'll make that offer to someone else. I have the lawyer
here for the necessary paperwork. Once you sign custody
over to W…to Miss Maher.'

But it was a slip. The start of Wendy's name… It made
Sonia lift her eyes from the cheque and she stared from
Luke to Wendy, and then they stayed on Wendy.

And it was impossible for Wendy to take the hope from
her face fast enough. Oh, God…

And Sonia knew.

'You're doing it for her,' the woman spat. 'You're doing
it so *she* gets the kid. *She* wants her.' Her vindictiveness was
dreadful to see. What had happened in the past to cause this
hate? Who knew, but it was there and it was real. 'No! Two
hundred thousand? I'd spend it and then what? I'd have no
comeback on the kid at all. She'd be on Easy Street.'

She whirled and stared out the window. 'And look at
that?' She gestured to Nick's car, gleaming immaculately

out in the driveway, and her vitriol was increasing by the minute. 'We're worlds apart and I wanted that so much! My husband promised me we'd be rich, but he couldn't make it in a pink fit. Two hundred grand—and I'd guess it wouldn't even buy that. You must be loaded. It wouldn't make any difference to you at all, and the kid...'

'You can have the car, too—if you like.'

The sudden silence was deathly. You could have heard a pin drop. The entire room held its breath.

'You're...you're joking.' Unlike the cheque, the car was a real and tangible thing, gorgeous in its enticement, and Sonia's incredulous face told the room she knew its worth.

'I'm not joking.' Luke shrugged as if he was losing interest. 'The cheque and the car can both be yours. Now. The registration forms are in the glove compartment. I'm sure with these lawyers present I can sign it over on the spot. That's my last offer, though. Take it or leave it.'

The woman whirled to face him. Then she stared down at her daughter, and the indecision was written clearly on her face.

This wasn't tearing affection, though. It was still a desire to hurt.

But...the expensive car. And a cheque like this...

'If I sign...?'

'You need to be very clear,' Tom interrupted from behind her, and his voice was tainted with weariness—longstanding disillusionment with human nature. 'The money and the car have nothing to do with the adoption. Because the pre-adoptive time is up, if you sign now then your daughter is legally relinquished. You can arrange supervised access, but you'll have no further control.'

'But...I can sign now. I can drive the car away.'

'Yes. But you'll drive away alone.'

The woman closed her eyes for a long moment, and there was a trace of triumph in the flush on her hard cheeks.

Then she put a hand behind Gabbie's back and shoved her forward, back to Wendy. Decision made.

'You take her,' she said harshly. 'I never wanted her. I hated her father and I hate her. Just show me where to sign and I never want to see her again.'

Wendy left the men to it.

While Sonia signed form after form of relinquishment, and Luke signed over his precious car, she gathered Gabbie in her arms. She took her outside and cradled her as if she'd never let her go.

As she wouldn't.

'You're to forget your mum told us any of the horrid things that were said in there,' she said fiercely, hugging her so tight she thought she'd squash her. 'Your mummy and your daddy fought, and she's taking that anger out on you. But she's done the best thing she can possibly do for you. The loveliest thing for a mummy to do when she can't take care of you herself. She's given you to me. Did you hear what she said in there? She's given you up for adoption, Gabbie, and now you can be my little girl for ever. For ever and for ever and for ever.

'I can stay with you and Grace and Bruce?'

'You can stay with me and Grace and Bruce.'

'And...' Gabbie pushed herself back and gazed at Wendy with eyes that were big and bright with wonder '...Luke gave his beautiful car to Mummy so she'd give me to you.'

She'd understood that much. Wendy smiled at her with eyes that were glistening with tears.

'Yes, he did.'

'Do you think...?' Gabbie said seriously '...do you think Luke loves us?'

'I think he must,' Wendy said tremulously. 'I think he must a lot and a lot and a lot.'

CHAPTER ELEVEN

HE'D left.

Wendy had heard the cars departing. First the Aston Martin, gunned down the road by an inexpert hand. She'd hoped Sonia had organised insurance—and then had been tempted enough to hope that maybe she hadn't. Then there had been the sound of two other cars. That would take care of Nick and the city lawyers, she'd thought. But when she'd taken Gabbie back inside she'd found Nick and Tom waiting for her.

No Luke.

'Congratulations, young lady,' Tom told Gabbie gravely, and the flushed look on his face told Wendy he couldn't have been more pleased at this ending. 'We've just organised you a new mother. Nick has the legal forms here, and if you'd like to sign them, Wendy, we can get things underway.' He grinned. 'You realise, you'll have to submit to social security checks as an adoptive mother.' And then he chuckled. 'If I have to forge them myself they'll be fantastic. Well done.'

'Where's Luke?' Wendy asked.

'He's driven Sonia's car into the second-hand car dealer in Bay Beach,' Nick told her, his eyes resting on her face. 'The agreement is that we'll send the proceeds on to her straight away.'

'And...and then?'

'I guess he's going back to Sydney.'

Without seeing her? Wendy's heart sank to her boots.

'I need to see him,' she said desperately. 'Nick, I need to catch him.'

He smiled. 'Now, how did I know you'd say that? As it happens, I'm available to take this little lady out to the farm.' He stooped to Gabbie's height. 'Gabbie, you know that Shanni and Harry are at the farm looking after Grace and Bruce while Wendy's here with you. Wendy needs to see Luke—to say thank you for what he did for you both today. Do you agree with that?'

Gabbie considered. Things were going very right for once in her small world, and her smile said she could afford to be generous. 'Yes,' she said.

'Then, if Wendy goes to look for Luke, will you come back to the farm with me?'

'And you'll come back, as well?' she asked Wendy, and Wendy nodded.

'As soon as I've found Luke.'

'Tell him we love him, too,' Gabbie said, and, amazingly, she tucked her hand into Nick's and she smiled and smiled. 'Okay. Let's go home. I need to tell Bruce that I can stay with him for ever.'

He was still there.

Bay Beach Motors was right on the esplanade. Wendy pulled up and Sonia's car was parked on the tarmac and Luke was waiting patiently while a sales rep crawled all over it.

'Eight hundred dollars,' the man was saying as Wendy approached. 'It's a wreck. That's the best I can do.'

'Fine.' Luke looked drawn and haggard. The flights and the stress were starting to get to him. He put his hand in his pocket, withdrew his wallet and handed over a roll of bank notes. 'Here's another five hundred. Make a cheque out for one thousand three hundred dollars to Mrs Sonia

Rolands and we'll say that's what you paid us. That way she can't have any comeback on us. We've been more than generous.'

'You have been at that.' The salesman stared. 'She'll never expect this much.'

'Well, maybe it's her lucky day.' And then he turned as he heard Wendy approach behind him, and his face stilled at the sight of her.

'Hi,' she said.

He didn't smile. He just stood—waiting.

And so did the salesman. There must have been something about the tension between them—the vibes emanating from each—that made him stop and stare.

Maybe a more sensitive sort of guy might have melted into the background, but this salesman was going nowhere. He stared from Wendy to Luke and back again, and there was nothing for Wendy to do but what she'd intended to do all along—in broad daylight with whoever watching that wanted to.

She walked straight over to Luke, she took his face between her hands and she pulled his mouth down to hers to kiss him.

The kiss went on and on. First it was Wendy kissing Luke—he was so stunned that he was almost rigid. But she kissed on, her soft lips pleading, and the warm sunlight played over their joined faces and the salesman looked on in wonder—and Luke couldn't resist for ever.

She felt his tension slacken in his body and a tremor ran right through him. She felt him begin to respond. Please...

And then she wasn't kissing him any more. She was being kissed herself—with a thoroughness and ruthlessness and hunger that left her breathless.

Her Luke...

Finally it ended. Somehow it must, though afterwards

she could never tell how long that wondrous, healing kiss had lasted. Ten minutes? Longer? No matter.

They pulled away and their audience had expanded. There were now three sales reps watching with avid interest, and a motley group of tourists on the esplanade were gazing on with blatant approval.

It didn't matter one bit. Luke held her at arm's length and he smiled at her with the smile she loved so much it made her heart still within her breast. Her Luke... Please, still her Luke.

'Was that a thank-you kiss?' he asked in a voice that was none too steady. It was a husky whisper, and it was laced with pure desire.

'No.' She shook her head, her eyes devouring him with love. 'It was an *I love you* kiss. It was an *I'm sorry, and I've been a fool and I want you more than I ever wanted anyone in my life* kiss. I love you so much, my wonderful Luke. I want you to marry me. If you...if you'll still have me.'

Silence. He took it in—he took all of her in—and the silence went on and on.

And then...

'I might well buy another sports car,' he said, eyeing her speculatively as if the thought had just come to him out of left field.

She grinned at that. 'Do you have any money left?'

'Not a lot.' He sighed. 'I'll just have to make more. I need a quiet room where I can concentrate though—a farm, maybe—and a nice, peaceful family environment...'

'Family?' She chuckled, a lovely, joyous sound that rang over the foreshore. 'I think I can manage family. I have a baby at hand. Also a five-year-old, a half-grown basset pup, the odd hundred or so cows and, as of last week, twenty new point-of-lay hens.' She chuckled and her eyes devoured him with all the love in the world. 'How does that sound?'

'I have another leather jacket in my baggage,' he warned her. 'All the way from Fifth Avenue.'

'How very suitable,' she said, and her loving gaze didn't falter. 'In case we get another crow for you to rescue.'

'And if we don't?'

'You wear it and I'll love you wearing it,' she told him. Her smile faded. 'Luke, I've been really, really stupid...'

He put a finger on her lips, but there were still tests for her to pass. He gazed around the parking lot at the shining cars lined up for sale. 'There's a beaut little red roadster over there,' he said thoughtfully. 'I think I fancy it—right now.'

'I thought you said you were broke.'

'Comparatively,' he said, and took her into his arms and nestled his chin into her hair. 'Compared to yesterday.'

'So if you really wanted that little red roadster...'

'I guess it wouldn't break the bank.' And then he put her away from him for a little and gazed at her. 'How about you? How would you feel about me buying it?'

'I love what you love,' she said simply. 'Now and for ever. You want a roadster, you buy a roadster. Luke, until that moment in the office when you just said calmly, ''You can have the car, too,'' I never believed...'

'That I wasn't like Adam?'

'That you were nothing like Adam. That I could trust you always, with whatever I had.'

'With you?'

The words were simply said, and they came from the heart. Around them, their audience was growing by every appreciative minute. Bay Beach was seeing a romance at its best here, and they were soaking up every minute of it.

There were those here who knew Wendy and who

wished her joy, but there were those who were strangers and knew they didn't have to wish for anything. Joy was plainly written on two wondering faces. Here was a happy ending—or a truly wonderful beginning.

'I'll trust you for ever,' Wendy said, her eyes glistening with unshed tears. 'Oh, Luke, how could I have been so blind?'

'A minor error of judgement I'm prepared to overlook,' he said expansively. 'Did you sign your mothering agreement? Do you have legal rights to Gabbie?'

'Yes.'

'And I signed my car away. It's a day for signing if ever I saw one.'

'I guess...'

'What's the legal timeframe for getting married in this country?' he demanded suddenly, and his eyes glinted with love and laughter.

'A month is the minimum. If we sign our intentions now.'

'Then, that's what we'll do,' he said softly, and he took her hands in his and he kissed her again so deeply that all the world knew they were seeing a marriage—right at this very moment. From now on, these two were one. 'Right now, while we're in a signing mood, we'll sign our intentions to stay together for ever. What do you say, my love?'

And there was nothing she could say—not for quite a while until that sealing kiss came to an end. When finally he released her—but not very far—she stood back and smiled and smiled and smiled.

'Yes, love,' she told him. 'I'll sign anything you want. And then?'

'And then we concentrate on living happily ever after,' he told her solemnly. 'Just you and me and Gabbie and Grace and Bruce...and whoever else comes along.'

'Whoever...?'

'You've no objection to expanding our family just a little?' he asked. 'You can get some very big sports cars these
days.'

'Oh, yeah, with dinky baby seats and the works. I'll bet.'
But she was laughing.

'If you pay enough you can get them specially made.'
His eyes held hers in the sunlight and they didn't leave her
for a moment. 'But a baby would be perfect, I think. We
started this whole deal with a baby bargain, my love. What
better way to seal it—but with a baby.'

'Or six?'

'*Six!*'

'Or whoever comes along,' she said serenely. 'Let's just
wait and see, my love. Let's just see what love brings.'

What happens when you suddenly discover your happy twosome is about to be turned into a...*family*?
Do you laugh?
Do you cry?
Or...do you get married?

The answer is all of the above—and plenty more!

Share the laughter and the tears with
Harlequin Romance® as these
unsuspecting couples have to be

When parenthood takes you by surprise!

THE BACHELOR'S BABY
Liz Fielding (August, #3666)

CLAIMING HIS BABY
Rebecca Winters (October, #3673)

HER HIRED HUSBAND
Renee Roszel (December, #3681)

Available wherever Harlequin books are sold.

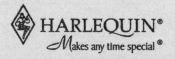

HARLEQUIN®
Makes any time special ®

Visit us at www.eHarlequin.com   HRREADY2

If you enjoyed what you just read,
then we've got an offer you can't resist!

Take 2 bestselling love stories FREE!

Plus get a FREE surprise gift!

Clip this page and mail it to Harlequin Reader Service®

IN U.S.A.
3010 Walden Ave.
P.O. Box 1867
Buffalo, N.Y. 14240-1867

IN CANADA
P.O. Box 609
Fort Erie, Ontario
L2A 5X3

YES! Please send me 2 free Harlequin Romance® novels and my free surprise gift. After receiving them, if I don't wish to receive anymore, I can return the shipping statement marked cancel. If I don't cancel, I will receive 6 brand-new novels every month, before they're available in stores! In the U.S.A., bill me at the bargain price of $3.15 plus 25¢ shipping & handling per book and applicable sales tax, if any*. In Canada, bill me at the bargain price of $3.59 plus 25¢ shipping & handling per book and applicable taxes**. That's the complete price and a savings of 10% off the cover prices—what a great deal! I understand that accepting the 2 free books and gift places me under no obligation ever to buy any books. I can always return a shipment and cancel at any time. Even if I never buy another book from Harlequin, the 2 free books and gift are mine to keep forever.

186 HEN DC7K
386 HEN DC7L

Name _____ (PLEASE PRINT)

Address _____ Apt.#

City _____ State/Prov. _____ Zip/Postal Code

* Terms and prices subject to change without notice. Sales tax applicable in N.Y.
** Canadian residents will be charged applicable provincial taxes and GST.
   All orders subject to approval. Offer limited to one per household and not valid to
   current Harlequin Romance® subscribers.
   ® are registered trademarks of Harlequin Enterprises Limited.

HROM01   ©2001 Harlequin Enterprises Limited

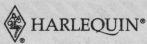

HARLEQUIN®

makes any time special—online...

eHARLEQUIN.com

your romantic life

—Romance 101———————
♥ Guides to romance, dating and flirting.

—Dr. Romance ———————
♥ Get romance advice and tips from
our expert, Dr. Romance.

—Recipes for Romance———
♥ How to plan romantic meals for you
and your sweetie.

—Daily Love Dose————————
♥ Tips on how to keep the romance
alive every day.

—Tales from the Heart———
♥ Discuss romantic dilemmas with other
members in our Tales from the Heart
message board.

All this and more available at
www.eHarlequin.com
on Women.com Networks

HINTL1R

Harlequin truly does make any time special. . . . This year we are celebrating weddings in style!

A Walk Down the Aisle

WEDDING CELEBRATION

To help us celebrate, we want you to tell us how wearing the Harlequin wedding gown will make your wedding day special. As the grand prize, Harlequin will offer one lucky bride the chance to **"Walk Down the Aisle"** in the Harlequin wedding gown!

There's more...

For her honeymoon, she and her groom will spend five nights at the **Hyatt Regency Maui.** As part of this five-night honeymoon at the hotel renowned for its romantic attractions, the couple will enjoy a candlelit dinner for two in Swan Court, a sunset sail on the hotel's catamaran, and duet spa treatments.

A HYATT RESORT AND SPA

Maui • Molokai • Lanai

To enter, please write, in, 250 words or less, how wearing the Harlequin wedding gown will make your wedding day special. The entry will be judged based on its emotionally compelling nature, its originality and creativity, and its sincerity. This contest is open to Canadian and U.S. residents only and to those who are 18 years of age and older. There is no purchase necessary to enter. Void where prohibited. See further contest rules attached. Please send your entry to:

Walk Down the Aisle Contest

In Canada
P.O. Box 637
Fort Erie, Ontario
L2A 5X3

In U.S.A.
P.O. Box 9076
3010 Walden Ave.
Buffalo, NY 14269-9076

You can also enter by visiting www.eHarlequin.com
Win the Harlequin wedding gown and the vacation of a lifetime!
The deadline for entries is October 1, 2001.

HARLEQUIN®
Makes any time special ®

PHWDACONT1

HARLEQUIN WALK DOWN THE AISLE TO MAUI CONTEST 1197
OFFICIAL RULES
NO PURCHASE NECESSARY TO ENTER

1. To enter, follow directions published in the offer to which you are responding. Contest begins April 2, 2001, and ends on October 1, 2001. Method of entry may vary. Mailed entries must be postmarked by October 1, 2001, and received by October 8, 2001.

2. Contest entry may be, at times, presented via the Internet, but will be restricted solely to residents of certain geographic areas that are disclosed on the Web site. To enter via the Internet, if permissible, access the Harlequin Web site (www.eHarlequin.com) and follow the directions displayed online. Online entries must be received by 11:59 p.m. E.S.T. on October 1, 2001.

   In lieu of submitting an entry online, enter by mail by hand-printing (or typing) on an 8½" x 11" plain piece of paper, your name, address (including zip code), Contest number/name and in 250 words or fewer, why winning a Harlequin wedding dress would make your wedding day special. Mail via first-class mail to: Harlequin Walk Down the Aisle Contest 1197, (in the U.S.) P.O. Box 9076, 3010 Walden Avenue, Buffalo, NY 14269-9076, (in Canada) P.O. Box 637, Fort Erie, Ontario L2A 5X3, Canada.

   Limit one entry per person, household address and e-mail address. Online and/or mailed entries received from persons residing in geographic areas in which Internet entry is not permissible will be disqualified.

3. Contests will be judged by a panel of members of the Harlequin editorial, marketing and public relations staff based on the following criteria:

   - Originality and Creativity—50%
   - Emotionally Compelling—25%
   - Sincerity—25%

   In the event of a tie, duplicate prizes will be awarded. Decisions of the judges are final.

4. All entries become the property of Torstar Corp. and will not be returned. No responsibility is assumed for lost, late, illegible, incomplete, inaccurate, nondelivered or misdirected mail or misdirected e-mail, for technical, hardware or software failures of any kind, lost or unavailable network connections, or failed, incomplete, garbled or delayed computer transmission or any human error which may occur in the receipt or processing of the entries in this Contest.

5. Contest open only to residents of the U.S. (except Puerto Rico) and Canada, who are 18 years of age or older, and is void wherever prohibited by law; all applicable laws and regulations apply. Any litigation within the Province of Quebec respecting the conduct or organization of a publicity contest may be submitted to the Régie des alcools, des courses et des jeux for a ruling. Any litigation respecting the awarding of a prize may be submitted to the Régie des alcools, des courses et des jeux only for the purpose of helping the parties reach a settlement. Employees and immediate family members of Torstar Corp. and D. L. Blair, Inc., their affiliates, subsidiaries and all other agencies, entities and persons connected with the use, marketing or conduct of this Contest are not eligible to enter. Taxes on prizes are the sole responsibility of winners. Acceptance of any prize offered constitutes permission to use winner's name, photograph or other likeness for the purposes of advertising, trade and promotion on behalf of Torstar Corp., its affiliates and subsidiaries without compensation to the winner, unless prohibited by law.

6. Winners will be determined no later than November 15, 2001, and will be notified by mail. Winners will be required to sign and return an Affidavit of Eligibility form within 15 days after winner notification. Noncompliance within that time period may result in disqualification and an alternative winner may be selected. Winners of trip must execute a Release of Liability prior to ticketing and must possess required travel documents (e.g. passport, photo ID) where applicable. Trip must be completed by November 2002. No substitution of prize permitted by winner. Torstar Corp. and D. L. Blair, Inc., their parents, affiliates, and subsidiaries are not responsible for errors in printing or electronic presentation of Contest, entries and/or game pieces. In the event of printing or other errors which may result in unintended prize values or duplication of prizes, all affected game pieces or entries shall be null and void. If for any reason the Internet portion of the Contest is not capable of running as planned, including infection by computer virus, bugs, tampering, unauthorized intervention, fraud, technical failures, or any other causes beyond the control of Torstar Corp. which corrupt or affect the administration, secrecy, fairness, integrity or proper conduct of the Contest, Torstar Corp. reserves the right, at its sole discretion, to disqualify any individual who tampers with the entry process and to cancel, terminate, modify or suspend the Contest or the Internet portion thereof. In the event of a dispute regarding an online entry, the entry will be deemed submitted by the authorized holder of the e-mail account submitted at the time of entry. Authorized account holder is defined as the natural person who is assigned to an e-mail address by an Internet access provider, online service provider or other organization that is responsible for arranging e-mail address for the domain associated with the submitted e-mail address. **Purchase or acceptance of a product offer does not improve your chances of winning.**

7. Prizes: (1) Grand Prize—A Harlequin wedding dress (approximate retail value: $3,500) and a 5-night/6-day honeymoon trip to Maui, HI, including round-trip air transportation provided by Maui Visitors Bureau from Los Angeles International Airport (winner is responsible for transportation to and from Los Angeles International Airport) and a Harlequin Romance Package, including hotel accomodations (double occupancy) at the Hyatt Regency Maui Resort and Spa, dinner for (2) two at Swan Court, a sunset sail on Kiele V and a spa treatment for the winner (approximate retail value: $4,000); (5) Five runner-up prizes of a $1000 gift certificate to selected retail outlets to be determined by Sponsor (retail value $1000 ea.). Prizes consist of only those items listed as part of the prize. Limit one prize per person. All prizes are valued in U.S. currency.

8. For a list of winners (available after December 17, 2001) send a self-addressed, stamped envelope to: Harlequin Walk Down the Aisle Contest 1197 Winners, P.O. Box 4200 Blair, NE 68009-4200 or you may access the www.eHarlequin.com Web site through January 15, 2002.

Contest sponsored by Torstar Corp., P.O. Box 9042, Buffalo, NY 14269-9042, U.S.A.

PHWDACONT2